Praise for Abandon All Hope

Eric Freeman toils for a Chicago-based educational software company now run by the Japanese. Habitually unemployed Evan Jarrett shovels snow to earn money while working on his magnum opus, *The Positive Life*. They are at the forefront of the gallery of 90's-era fringe dwellers – immigrants, recluses, "alcoholic layabouts", among many others – that inhabit Scott Spires' wry, perceptive, and provocative novel.

Abandon All Hope's deceptively mundane storyline rewards the reader on two levels. Frequent visits are made to the Book Bunker (used books) and Vic's Vinyl (used LP's). On a more abstract level, the likes of Cervantes and Blake, Mahler and Bruckner, serve as tutelary presences in the novel's background. There is the humor of characters' names – Beefheart, Hotchkiss, Latour, Gumm, Frumkin. Yet each bears some aspect of Spires' vision of a tenuous, even fragile, freedom on the fringes of an "acceptable" society which itself may be an illusion. His clean wry prose touches on the fringe dweller within us all.

Abandon All Hope is a grin-on-your-way-to-the-gallows book. And smile you will. But smile too much and you will miss the insights into American culture that illumine Scott Spires' novel. Though set in the Chicago of the late 90's, *Abandon All Hope's* prescient shadows extend all too tellingly into the America of today.

— Harry Ringel, author of *Shemhazai's Game* and *The Phantom of Skid Row*

More Praise for *Abandon All Hope*

What Tom Wolfe achieved in the last decades of the twentieth century for Manhattan in *The Bonfire of the Vanities* and Atlanta in *A Man in Full*, Scott Spires has succeeded doing for Chicago in the late 1990's with his novel, *Abandon All Hope*. Moreover, Spires has provided not one, but two, equally compelling protagonists seeking to bring meaning to their lives as they struggle in a society and culture in which neither feels they belong.

The world the two protagonists inhabit, filled with diverse and sometimes quirky characters, makes for an entertaining and thought-provoking examination of the human condition of which we are all a part.

 —Richard D. Bank, author of *The Tree of Sorrow:*
Growing Up In The Shadow of the Holocaust and
I Am Terezin.

Abandon All Hope

A Novel

Scott Spires

www.auctuspublishers.com

Chapter 1.

Snow Day

Like a drunk who wants to tell you his life story, winter just won't let go of us, thought Eric Freeman as he looked out his bedroom window.

There was something about the glare of the light filtering into his apartment, the feeling of stillness, the silence. He thanked a God he didn't quite believe in that it was Sunday and he didn't have to go anywhere. The deadness of the day began to bother him while he was making breakfast, so he switched on the TV in the living room to have some company. The usual story, the one that had dominated the airwaves for the past couple of months, was moving into a new phase. As Eric finished pouring his coffee, he heard a stentorian male voice booming from the box: "Mr. President, Kathleen Willey says you made unwanted sexual advances towards her, and that directly contradicts your testimony. You can't both be telling the truth, can you?"

The President responded, "Well, I don't know what she said, because I didn't see the interview last night, but I can tell you this: ever since this story came out months ago – and as you know, this story has been in three different in-carnations – I have said that nothing improper happened..."

Eric sat down to watch the spectacle, digging into his bowl of Quisp, the saucer-shaped sugary cereal – a rare treat he had never been able to find in Chicago, but which a friend of his had brought back from a business trip to the East Coast. He enjoyed watching Mr. Clinton weave and dodge his way through this scandal, a master of the rhetorical arts of self-defense. *Smooth,* just like this coffee, he thought. "I am mystified and disappointed by this turn of events." An excellent line, he thought. But he began to lose interest when another one of the reporters – obviously some high-minded busybody – asked, "Mr. President, can I suggest that we get on with the important topic of what our children are going to be doing in the next century, in science and math?" The other attendees burst into applause, at which point Eric concluded that no more free entertainment would be forthcoming, at least on this broadcast.

He changed the channel. The usual talking heads filled the screen, putting their best positive or negative spin on what the President of these United States had said during his most recent grilling. Eric decided that this was as good a time as any to revisit the bathroom. He fumbled through a small pile of publications stacked on his coffee table, looking for a "crapworthy" article, something that could help him pass the time agreeably while sitting on the toilet. Five minutes of amusement was the goal. He picked up the free local newspaper, serving the lakefront neighborhoods of Lakeview, Uptown, and Edgewater, and turned to the police report. Seated, he read about Arthur F., who had stolen a

6

bagful of dog collars from a pet shop; Louis W., who had "behaved indecently" by masturbating on a park bench in broad daylight; and a teenager (name withheld) found in possession of twenty-one cell phones, none of whose numbers she was able to give. A line from Kant went through Eric's head: "From such crooked timber as man is made, nothing exactly straight can be formed."

Finished. Out in the living room, the TV was still on; Eric lowered the volume and reclined on the couch. He was not tired, but he wasn't energetic either. He didn't feel particularly good, but on the other hand, he didn't feel too bad. He wasn't happy, but you couldn't say he was sad. Everything evened out. A recipe for paralysis, he mused, for the whole goddam day. Plants must feel like this.

Yet he was upset, because this was how he usually felt at work, at Eldritch EduWare out in the western suburbs, where he sat in a cubicle all day with half his brain focused on work and the other half on what he would rather be doing, which was a lot of things. Now, none of those things attracted him. On Saturday he had been at Vic's Vinyl, where he'd picked up a couple of items, including a rare recording of Javanese gamelan music as well as a "half-speed mastered" LP of Pierre Boulez conducting Stravinsky (*The Rite of Spring*, with the Cleveland Orchestra, made in 1969), but he wasn't up to listening to them now.

The gray gloom he was sitting in didn't make things better. He switched on a lamp. With a *twnk!* the light bulb announced its demise. Eric rummaged in the kitchen for a new one. Damn, I'm out! No choice but to head out into the cold in search of illumination. He was thrilled to have a reason to do something.

He threw on his coat, made his way down two flights of stairs, and opened the front door of his building onto a fresh white world. A still, icy blue sky stretched over the rows of houses and apartment buildings like a dome of crystal;

gray steam and smoke from chimneys drifted upwards. The caretakers of the building next door – stocky red-faced Mary in her big puffy coat, and her little beige dog Trevor – were out already, sweeping away the snow.

Eric struggled and trudged, trudged and struggled along the sidewalk, snow already partially tramped down under multitudes of feet. Although he was in pretty good shape, he found it taxing, like wading through seaweed. As he pushed his way forward, a memory popped open in his mind. It was his brother-in-law, Porter Hotchkiss, who lived in the northern suburb of Glenview and worked as an "industrial psychologist," a profession which mystified Eric. Porter was saying, in his smug, smiley way, "Yes, Eric, but what have you got to show for it?"

Broadway, normally busy, was mostly empty of traffic today. Eric turned left. The film in his mind rewound and started playing from the beginning, as it had many times already. It was a memory from a family gathering on the previous New Year's Eve, when Eric had been having dinner with Porter and Nora Hotchkiss at their home. The Hotchkisses were in their late thirties, a few years older than Eric. The topic of Eric's refusal to commit to anything with implications of permanence – buying a house, marrying a woman, raising a child, following a profession – somehow came up. Eric defended himself by pointing to his freedom, the lack of emotional or financial burdens, and the possibility of sleeping late on weekends. After he delivered this little speech (which he knew sounded a little arrogant), Porter made his smug riposte.

There had long been a bit of covert hostility between them, nothing really serious, just a tension arising from their basic dissimilarity. Porter fit the template of an upwardly mobile, dedicated professional suburban dad. He also liked to watch sports on TV, took self-help books seriously, and ate at family-oriented theme restaurants. Eric

hated televised sports, thought self-help books were for
chumps who couldn't help themselves, and was suspicious
of any restaurant where the theme was more important
than the food. Porter enjoyed mocking Eric's interests and
pretensions. This comeback was not a surprise to Eric. Yet
it lodged in him like a bee's stinger.

He entered Dominick's, planning to buy some food as
well. Light bulbs, what else should I get? Milk always a good
idea, maybe some canned tuna, a few cans of soup, the usual
bachelor provisions...Porter and Nora had something to
show for their years of work: a nice house, two kids (Brent,
six and Lianna, three), two cars, memberships in clubs that
counted, the means to hire a Guatemalan maid to take care
of the kids along with Nora, who had cut back drastically
on her law practice in order to spend more time at home.

Eric's reply to Porter's question had been a frivolous one,
something about the important role he played keeping ethnic restaurants and used book, record and clothing stores
in business. In fact he had no satisfactory answer, and that
disturbed him.

As he exited the supermarket, Eric saw a young man
coming towards him. He was tall and gawky, with glasses.
In fact, except for the glasses, he looked like a more atten-
uated, younger, and hungrier version of Eric: a bit taller, a
bit thinner, a bit paler. A woolen cap covered the top half
of his head. He was carrying a snow shovel. He looked at
Eric rather earnestly. "Excuse me," he said.

"Yes?"

"You need your car cleared, or your door or sidewalk? I'm
offering my services."

Eric took about two seconds to evaluate this guy.
Couldn't be older than twenty-five; delicate, intelligent
looks; clean, plainly not drunk. A serious, entrepreneurial
individual. Maybe a college student looking to pick up a few
extra bucks? "How much do you charge?"

"Ten bucks to fully dig out a car, create a space for it. Five if you just want some space in front of your door, or a clean sidewalk."

"I don't have a car," said Eric.

"Sidewalk?"

"That needs shoveling, but I can do it myself."

The guy stared at him. The earnest look didn't go away.

"Thanks anyway," said Eric, trying to put some finality into his voice. He walked away.

Home again: the brown brick apartment building with its heavy moat of snow. Eric went inside, up to his apartment on the third floor, to replace the lightbulb and put away his other purchases in the kitchen. What about Eldritch? he thought. Didn't he have something to show for several years of work there? Kids were learning to read, somewhere in this country, using a textbook he had helped to write, and the accompanying CD-ROM which familiarized them with such concepts as nouns (*shoes*), adjectives (*athletic shoes*), even phrasal verbs (*Take those athletic shoes off!*). In fact Eric disliked kids, but thankfully they didn't stay kids forever, and literacy was a good cause, he thought as he screwed the new bulb into the lamp.

Yet such triumphs were fleeting and rare. So much of work was merely a struggle, vast energy expended for meager returns, like plowing a field with a fork. An amiable charlatan, Woody Latour, sat atop Eric's department, and atop Woody sat a Japanese management whose understanding of Eldritch's function and market was, to put it charitably, still in the learning stages. Recently a ghastly rumor had begun to circulate to the effect that the management was planning to hold a contest for the writing of a company song. No one Eric asked could confirm this, but neither did they deny it.

A rhythmic scraping, coming from outside, interrupted these gloomy thoughts. Eric went to the front window. The young man he had seen just a few minutes earlier was cleaning the sidewalk with his big shovel.

Eric came out and stood at a safe distance, watching the guy finish up. He went at his work very methodically, shove-scoop-toss, shove-scoop-toss, with the urgency of an army technician trying to repair something while under fire. He threw the final shovelful of snow to the side, then stood straight and pioneer-like on the clean sidewalk, shovel in his hand and red in his face.

"I said I could do it myself," said Eric.

"You needed it," said the guy.

"Thanks, but..."

"In case you're wondering, it's free. I'm not a squeegee man; I'm not trying to trap you into paying. I did it because you needed it."

Eric took a few steps closer. "Why did you do it?"

"Because you needed it."

Eric came closer. "Really?"

"Really."

Eric thought for a second. "Okay, why did you *really* do it?"

"Because you needed it," repeated the guy.

Eric looked at him closely. *"Really?"*

"Yes."

Standing there with his hands stuffed into his pockets, Eric became conscious of the cold and was starting to feel stiff and uncomfortable. "Did you do it for the exercise?"

"No," he said with a smile, "I did it because you needed it."

"You don't even know me."

"So what?"

"Do you go around the city doing favors for strangers?"

"When I've met my basic needs, then I can think about doing favors for people."

"But why me?"

"Because you—"

"Thanks, I knew the answer already. Can I ask you something else?"

"Go ahead."

"And please don't say because I needed it. What are you doing? I mean, is this a business or what? Is this a form of advertising?"

"No," said the young man. "I have my reasons for doing this. It would take a little while to explain it to you. As for business, well, I have to do something to support myself. I wish I didn't have to worry about money, but don't we all."

Eric became conscious of the aroma of cooking – sausages, pancakes, bacon – wafting towards him on the light breeze from the Lakefront Diner on the corner. The late-breakfast crowd was there now, the get-up-late hedonists recovering from their Saturday debauchery. Eric's nose pushed his brain out of the way and made a proposal. "By the way, you feeling hungry?"

"Hungry? Why?"

"How'd you like it if I bought you something to eat? I'm heading to the diner on the corner, you can come along."

The guy smiled. "Sounds good. Thanks."

"Don't worry about it. What's your name, anyway?"

"Evan."

"I'm Eric. You live round here?"

"Edgewater."

That was about twenty blocks away. "How come you're here and not there?"

"Business is better here," said Evan. "People are more willing to pay. I've done seven shovel-jobs already today, made some money. That takes care of my basic needs."

People asking for help were common in the neighborhood. They asked for money ("so I can buy something to eat"), money ("so I can get home"), money ("so I can make a phone call"), directions, the time, "sign my petition," and so on. Usually Eric just walked on by. But this was the first time a person on the street had ever done a favor for him, and that deserved something in return.

Eric retrieved his coat from the apartment; when he came back out, Evan slung the shovel over his shoulder and followed Eric to the Lakefront Diner. It wasn't yet noon, and there were still some free seats. Evan stood his shovel next to the coat rack at the entrance. "This has to be where I can keep an eye on it," he said. "It's my livelihood." They sat down at one of the booths by the window, where they got a good view of pedestrians struggling through the snow.

"Have whatever you want," said Eric as he surveyed the menu. He decided on coffee and toast with some bacon on the side.

"Blueberry pancakes and coffee for me."

"Another breakfast, eh?"

"I need my energy."

They ordered. The clumsy new blond woman was waiting on them. Eric had talked to her a few times. She was about twenty-eight to thirty, tall, thin and a little awkward in her movements, as if she hadn't quite mastered the mechanics of balancing plates of food and cups full of hot liquid. He knew that her name was Alina, she came from Russia, she had been in this country for a few years, and that being a waitress in a diner was not a job she hoped to get when she first moved here. "I bring you guys coffee in a moment," she said, marching off to the kitchen.

More small talk (principally on the weather and the vagaries of the public transport system) followed, until Eric made a break for greater significance. "Listen Evan, since I'm buying you lunch, I want you to answer my question. What are you doing? What is it about, this shoveling, doing people favors and all that?"

Coffee arrived, and Evan sipped it with deliberation before answering. "The shoveling is one of the jobs I do. On a weekend like this, I can make two or three hundred, goes pretty far toward paying the rent. That's why I'm down here where people are willing to pay."

"Are you a student?" asked Eric.

"Was."

"You graduate?"

"Dropped out."

"So what do you do? I mean, just odd jobs like this?"

"Sometimes. I work when I have to. I live in an apartment that costs me less than four hundred a month. If I budget carefully, I can live on a few thousand dollars a year, doing temp jobs, and other jobs that I create myself, like this one." He stopped to sip his coffee.

"So what do you do with all that free time?"

Evan looked into the distance. "Well, right now I'm working on a scheme of calendrical reform. The way we classify time, and hence the way we use it, is inefficient. So I'm working on a way to fix things. I'm also writing a philosophical treatise. It's called *The Positive Life*."

"You don't say. What's the essence of the positive life? Shoveling snow for a living?"

"Hey, if it works for you," said Evan. "Shoveling snow can provide a very good living, if you have a deep commitment to it. But not many people do. No, the positive life is one of successful navigation."

"Successful navigation? Like a sailor?"

Evan laughed at Eric's apparent naivete. "Navigation through the possibilities that life throws in our way. Being intelligent enough to discern the most fruitful and satisfying possibilities."

"That sounds like common sense to me."

"In part it is. But first of all, common sense isn't all that common. And second, when we have to apply our sense in real life, it gets a lot more complex. That's why a system is needed. Most people don't have a system."

"You think so?" said Eric. "What about religion, ethics, all that stuff?"

"That's all important. But the type of system I'm trying to create is constructed from the ground up. I'm trying not to rely too much on things that already exist. Most people's systems are irrational. They don't examine the pre-existing elements closely enough."

Eric's probe was cut short by the arrival of the food. Evan dug into the pancakes with gusto. He looked so serious about them that Eric was afraid to interrupt him. He attacked the pancakes with a motion very similar to the one he had used on the snow, but instead of shove-scoop-toss, it was more like cut-stab-shove, cut-stab-shove, into his mouth, urgent like a dog but more methodical. Eric, playing with his own food, felt like a slacker.

After Evan had reduced the pancakes by about half of their volume, Eric asked: "Alright. Now can you answer my original question? Why did you clean my sidewalk?"

Evan put down his fork. "Because you needed it. I'm serious, that's not a frivolous answer. And as for your question, do I run around the city doing favors for people, well, that's a crude way of putting it, but I do. We need to change our priorities, our way of doing things, the way we relate to each other. I don't mean you and me, I mean all of us. All of humanity."

With his fingers, Eric was toying with the crust of his toast, breaking it down into tiny pieces. "So is this your philosophical system, or whatever you call it? *The Positive Vibe*, is that its name?"

"*The Positive Life*. That's part of it. It has to start small and grow from there. I shovel your walk, you shovel mine. After a while, in ten years or a hundred, we're all shoveling each other's walks, and we're doing it because it needs to be done, not because we hope to get something out of it." He picked up his fork and assaulted the pancakes again.

"So what's all this about calendar reform?" asked Eric.

"Mm," said Evan chewing, "I can't really explain that without showing you. I've got it all worked out on paper."

"Huh."

When lunch ended, Evan reached into his well-organized wallet, stuffed with five- and ten-dollar bills, and handed a card to Eric. "That's me." The contact info was there, under the words *Evan Jarrett. Philosopher & Activist.*

A world of strange people out there, thought Eric as he entered his apartment, feeling slightly more alive than when he had left it. Philosopher and activist? That was a new one. And what the hell was an industrial psychologist, anyway?

●

Back home, Eric lay on the couch, flipping randomly through the listings in the back of the *Chicago Reader*, surveying the arts and entertainment events, and amusing himself with the personal ads. The reason these people are still single, he figured, is that they make unrealistic demands. Here was one woman, all of 25 years old, who wouldn't even consider dating a man making less than $100,000 a year. Here was a guy who claimed to do physics *and* write poetry (hopefully not both at the same time), looking for a woman to be "his intellectual equal" yet also to "take care of him" when he needed it. This prospective mate should be between the ages of 21 and 24. Eric had never placed a personal ad of this type, but he began to wonder what he would say about himself if he did.

Part of the problem was that he lacked a purpose. In fact, he had always lacked a purpose. More specifically, he had toyed with a purpose now and then, but nothing ever stuck for very long. A series of snapshots of his life, taken at certain key moments, would bear this out. 1974: A very young Eric, enlisting his friends as actors and his mother as cinematographer, makes a ten-minute film about a voyage around the world. 1977: Eric has lost interest in directing films and has taken up astronomy. He spends cloudless evenings in the park near his suburban home, looking at planets through his telescope. 1980: Starting high school, he is instantly classified as a "nerd" by his classmates, even though he's lost interest in astronomy and science in general. He tries to combat this classification by playing sports, in which he does not excel. 1982: He goes on a trip to Asia and becomes interested in the region. 1989: He graduates from a respectable liberal arts college on the East Coast with a degree in Japanese history, having switched majors three times. He then spends the first few years of the 1990s wandering through Asia, Europe and the United States, teaching English and doing some writing and editing work for a company that specializes in catalogue software. 1995: Bored stiff with his catalogue job, he makes the switch to Eldritch EduWare, an educational publisher. The new job feels like an improvement; things don't start to go bad until 1997. In that year, the company is acquired by Tokyo-based Furuhashi Multimedia Concern, installs new upper management, and makes the decision to move the headquarters from downtown Chicago to the suburbs. Eric is dismayed by the new regime, and being a city-dweller, hates the new, long commute.

Which brings us to 1998. March was already at its halfway point, but the sky had dumped another thick blanket of white on Chicago and environs. If you're still looking for a purpose, maybe shoveling snow is the way to go? At least it gets you out into the world. Maybe he would feel better if he finally put on that record of Javanese gamelan music?

Chapter 2.

An Experiment in Living

Evan Jarrett needed oxygen to live. He breathed it in thousands of times a day, and then expelled it, mixed with carbon dioxide, exactly the same number of times. He needed food and drink, which he took into his body several times a day, at regular intervals. Also several times a day, the waste products of this nourishment were excreted from his body. Evan's brain took care of his cognitive functioning, while also regulating the motor functions of his body. In order to maintain his health and general well-being, Evan required an average of seven to eight hours of sleep every night.

One could extend this list of Evan's characteristics for several paragraphs before coming upon anything that was distinctive about him. In fact, Evan was starting to suspect that there was *nothing* distinctive about him. When he reflected upon this list, it seemed to him that so far in life, his only achievement was that he wasn't dead.

When he raised this issue with his parents for the first time, he was in high school. His parents dismissed his concerns by saying that nobody his age, with the exception of a few freaks and geniuses, had achieved anything. Evan couldn't argue with this, but hearing them say it, he realized that his problem was more complicated. In the absence of blinding talent and an obvious purpose in life, one needed a plan. It was a problem of defining, targeting, and achieving.

One day, his mother suggested a way forward. "Every day, first thing in the morning, accomplish some little thing. It could be cleaning your desk, or taking out the garbage. Shoveling snow. Or it could be solving a math problem that you haven't figured out yet. I know you've got a curious mind, that might work for you. Or reading a poem and finally understanding it. You do that, it'll give you confidence for the rest of the day."

Evan took this under advisement, as one of the numerous well-meaning pieces of advice he regularly got from adults. There was a solid core of good sense to it, however: methodical, repetitive action usually brought results. This was something he had seen in his own family life. His parents were both living incarnations of the wisdom they spouted: father had excelled in law school, and then as in-house counsel for a few companies; mother became a nurse. They knew everything about the importance of sticking to the plan, getting your work done, and passing certification.

High school, and his teenage years generally, had not been an easy experience for Evan. In a competitive suburban environment replete with pressure from parents, teachers, friends, and the school administration, it required both strength of will and some degree of cunning to distinguish oneself. Evan felt the pressure as much as any other student. He also genuinely wanted to carve out a niche for himself: to be admired, but more importantly, to be significant in some way. In a school where science whizzes, sports heroes, and class politicians snagged all the trophies and most of the attention, it was easy to feel like a loser. Evan got good grades for the most part, but he was no academic star. His name never featured in the local suburban paper, or in school announcements, where excellence was concerned. On the plus side, his name was never in the police blotter, but as an achievement this was merely negative. Socially, he was neither attractive to girls nor popular with boys. Being tall and a fast runner, he racked up a moderately impressive record on the track team; but outside of the Olympics, how many people watch or care about track-and-field events? It would be better to excel in football, basketball, or lacrosse, and he couldn't. He had talents in a few areas – a knack for abstract thinking and literary expression, a modicum of business savvy – but it wasn't clear to him how to manifest these talents in real life.

He read philosophers, at least their more accessible works. They offered him a way to acquire some perspective on his current condition, allowing him to get a more objective take on the circumstances he found himself in. Reading about people in different times and countries who had grappled with intractable issues made him feel that he had company. He dabbled in Nietzsche and Kierkegaard, had a brief flirtation with Spinoza, read a couple of the better-known effusions of the American Pragmatists, and got to know the Existentialists at second hand. During his junior year in high school, it struck him that a test of the will was in order. In his biology class, he was doing well. He had scored A's on the first two tests of the year. When the time for the third test arrived, Evan, whose mastery of the material was not in doubt, deliberately flunked it.

The biology teacher, Ms. Gumm, had been working at the school for twenty years, and had seen pretty much every problem, fixation, and quirk that students could bring into the classroom. Yet she had never seen anything quite like this. "Evan, you know the material. What on earth were you thinking?"

"I had to do it," he said. "I had to break the cycle somehow."

"Break what cycle? What are you talking about?"

"Forget it," said Evan. "Just give me my F. It's mine and I earned it."

Ms. Gumm offered Evan a way out. "Look, I know you could have gotten at least a B on that test. I'm so sure of this that you know what I'm going to do? I'm going to let you take the test again."

"Thanks, but no thanks. I earned that F!"

The argument continued. Ms. Gumm, following the protocol established for this kind of irregular behavior, got in touch with the school counselor. After some discussion, Evan agreed to retake the test, and received a B. He was glad that he had become such a cause for concern; it seemed like a tiny triumph in and of itself. He felt that he had succeeded in making his mark, and didn't really need that well-earned F after all.

The entire incident prompted Evan to meditate on the question of youthful rebellion. At the same time, he had acquired enough historical knowledge to know that youthful rebellions tend to take identical, imitative forms within each culture. Many students under the kind of pressure Evan was experiencing use bad academic performance as a form of protest, although they may not broadcast this fact quite as loudly as Evan did. Bad grades, like drugs, sexual promiscuity, and violent video games, were a stereotyped, unoriginal way to carve out one's identity. In the American suburban milieu, they were the default mode of rebellious teens. Evan didn't know any young people who were asserting an independent identity by becoming experts on the cinema of India, or by reviving crafts made obsolete by the Industrial Revolution, or by campaigning for a revival of the Austro-Hungarian Empire, or by immersing themselves in ancient Greek or Chinese thought. By itself, rebellion was not a form of distinction, and Evan was still failing to stand out from the crowd.

In some ways, Evan was a victim, a victim of the high expectations and the range of choices produced by modern industrial, consumer society – a society that had brought about wealth and security to a degree that had been unimaginable only a couple of generations previously. Once in his high school history class, the teacher was describing the crushing oppression and onerous burdens of being a peasant in Europe, a situation that persisted for centuries with little prospect of improvement. When the teacher finished, one of the boys – who was not known for manifesting intellectual curiosity – asked: "Well who would want to be a peasant?" There was no hint of sarcasm in his voice. Why be a peasant when you could run your own IT consulting firm instead?

As was usually the case for young people of his social class, high school was followed immediately by college. Since Evan had failed to stand out, he didn't bother to apply to the Ivies, the Little Ivies, the Public Ivies, or any other institution even remotely associated with the term "Ivy." Instead, he wound up at Eastbrook College, a respectable but not outstanding or famous liberal-arts institution in Wisconsin. Eastbrook was located in the Driftless Area in the southwestern part of the state, so called because it had escaped glaciation and its flattening effects. Consequently, it was hilly and forested, with deep river valleys and rocky outcrops; immigrants from Wales and Switzerland must have felt comforted by the familiarity of the landscape.

Evan, however, felt little comfort there. Mostly he felt lost, wondering what he was doing in this rural retreat.

Since philosophy had been an interest of his in high school, he decided to continue with it in college. One day his philosophy professor, Paul Frumkin, asked him to write an essay on "the social construction of reality." Dr. Frumkin was a hardcore Kantian, who believed that the world existed as an objective entity outside the minds of individuals, who made sense of the world by filtering this reality through their five senses. Evan, on the other hand, was sinking deeper into the conviction that reality did not exist as an objective entity, but was something "made up" by individuals as they went along, in accordance with their needs under certain circumstances. At the same time, he was beginning to take a more skeptical attitude to those thinkers he had once read: they hadn't really solved anything, so why should he continue reading them? Maybe it was time for him to strike out on his own intellectual path.

Paul Frumkin, like a lot of academics of his vintage – he was in his late forties – had precision-instrument spectacles and earnest long hair, but in other respects he seemed determined to rebel against being typecast as an introverted, refined intellectual. He never wore a tie to class, preferring casual clothes: flannel work shirts in winter, and T-shirts with messages, slogans, advertisements, or graphics in warmer weather. It wasn't unusual to see him lecturing on Hegel or Schopenhauer while wearing a T-shirt that urged *Nuke Unborn Gay Whales*. Sometimes he wore a jacket in some vulgar color, like magenta or canary yellow.

Evan's essay irritated Frumkin, who found it arrogant and dismissive; it failed to take contrary perspectives into account, even for the purpose of properly refuting them. Yet such was the passion of Evan's argument that Frumkin was intrigued enough to request a private meeting with Evan to discuss it. They got together in his office, where the professor asked the student if he believed that, before Copernicus propagated the theory of heliocentricity, the sun really *had* been revolving around the earth.

"Yes," said Evan.

"Why?"

"Because people believed it, and it gave their lives meaning."

"It gave their lives meaning, but it was false," stated Frumkin. He was wearing his yellow jacket over a T-shirt that advertised the extreme-metal band Napalm Death.

"It was true *because* it gave their lives meaning," insisted Evan. "The meaning is what makes it true."

"It sounds like what you're saying is that truth is a matter of practical application."

"No, I'm saying that truth is a function of meaning," said Evan. "If something really has meaning for you, you will act on it. Your action will have an effect. What's the point of truth if it has no effect in the world?"

"That's what I said," countered Frumkin. "Truth is a function of practical application, of action in the world. Which I don't believe myself, but which I think you do."

"It has to *mean* something first, before it gets practically applied," said Evan with some heat in his voice. "If it's not true, it won't have meaning to begin with."

"You might want to refine your perspective a bit," said Frumkin, trying to sound helpful. "Maybe you should read William James, or the other Pragmatists. They have a lot to say about this."

"I don't need to read anyone anymore to get ideas," said Evan. His face was reddening. "I get my ideas from thinking."

Frumkin started to say something, but stopped before anything significant came out of his mouth. He tried again. "Listen Evan, I don't think we're really that far apart."

Evan gave him a cold look. "Oh, yes we are."

Frumkin tried a different approach. "Evan, I don't normally come across a student paper that I genuinely want to discuss with its author. I've been around long enough to recognize all the tricks – copying of secondary sources, regurgitation of whatever I said in class without actually engaging with the subject matter at all. And nowadays, the kids are starting to copy their essays off the Internet, which is an even more brain-dead thing to do. So, when a student shows signs of independent thinking – as you have done here – I think it should be encouraged."

The conversation continued in this vein. Frumkin finally ended it by saying that, no matter how many ideas Evan was able to get "from thinking," it was a poor strategy to deliberately neglect what other great minds had thought about these issues. When Evan finally left the office, the professor looked winded and was smiling the way people do when they are glad to be extricated from an awkward social situation. Some while later, Evan dropped out of the college.

He tried again, attending classes at a community college near his house. Evan concentrated on film and photography, but after a couple of months dropped out due to boredom, and the realization that the visual arts were not the most promising venue for his creative imagination. At this point, his exasperated parents presented him with two options. If he wanted to continue living with them, he would have to pay rent, and do any chores around the house should that be necessary. His other option was to move out of the house and make his own way in the world while he decided on a career path. In order to steer him toward this second option, they offered him a lump sum starter payment to help him rent an apartment, a payment that they referred to as "seed capital." Beyond this, however, he would be responsible for his own maintenance. He took the second option.

Edgewater was affordable and decent. Before World War II it had been a fashionable area, so there were many elegant old apartment buildings left over from that time. This architectural legacy continued in the form of a strip of the lakefront dedicated to high-rise living; further inland were several sub-neighborhoods, such as the yuppie-dominated former Swedish enclave of Andersonville, and a number of worthwhile ethnic restaurants (many of them Middle Eastern or Asian, reflecting current patterns of immigration and settlement). The neighborhood also contained an unstable population of recent immigrants, college students, drifters, young professionals, and some people who just couldn't seem to get their lives together. Here and there, one also found old smashed cars parked on potholed streets, a few too many liquor stores, and a number of store-front religious structures, catering to adherents of the Full Gospel or the revelation of Mohammed. In short – it was a diverse area in every sense.

Shortly after he moved himself and his few possessions into a studio apartment in one of the cheaper buildings in the neighborhood, Evan had the revelation he had been waiting for. The city gave him a multitude of fresh, new stimuli that his safe, orderly, prosperous suburban environment had never hinted at. The world appeared to him as if torn into fragments that begged to be put together into some sort of coherent whole. The people Evan met bore this out. His neighbor, Isaiah, was a Nigerian immigrant who had arrived in the United States with a practically useless law degree from his home country, and was now reduced to working long hours at a Chinese fast-food joint to keep his head above water; a better life was a distant dream. Downstairs lived an old woman who never left her apartment, had no visitors, and never spoke to anyone. Her TV, usually tuned to either soap operas or talk shows, blared throughout the day. On the same floor as Evan lived Jeff and Nancy – he a disbarred lawyer, she an alcoholic layabout. Raging arguments would break out between them, sometimes punctuated by the throwing of objects. Across the street (so people said) lived a man who had served jail time for child molestation. These people might have existed in his previous suburban environment, but if so, they kept themselves (or were kept) out of sight. In the city, their presence was obvious. In the midst of all this, Evan also found himself free and out of the sight of any parental or scholastic authority for the first time that he could remember. It was an invigorating, vertiginous feeling. While living off his "seed capital," Evan looked for, and occasionally got, temporary jobs. Some were provided by a local agency, but on his own time, he noticed places that needed to be cleaned, or objects to be repaired, or similar minor gigs; basic handyman stuff, to which he could turn his entrepreneurial instincts.

An evening came when he was lying down on his bed after a particularly boring two-day job at a local factory, where he had spent the entire time packing pet supplies into boxes and taking the boxes out to a truck. It was the kind of repetitive job that people curse as an experience of enforced boredom and regimentation, but which, due to its very robotic nature, leaves the mind free to cogitate on other matters. As he lay on the bed, reflecting on the job and on his situation as a whole, certain half-developed thoughts arose with a fresh, hard clarity. The situation he found himself in – hell, his whole life – seemed to demand a response that went beyond either simple rejection or conventional forms of revolt. Material necessity itself, and the demands of society for a life of conformity, appeared to Evan as things to be opposed on a fundamental, almost biological level. Being trapped in materiality required the elevation and pursuit of a spiritual principle. And so, the thought struck Evan: he was here to conduct an experiment in living. His project would be idealistic and altruistic, meant to create a path that others could follow. All that bouncing and drifting here and there, between his home and college, between his studio apartment and the outside world: all this activity was leading to something significant, even if he hadn't understood it at the time. This experiment in living would be his road to distinction.

This notion captured his mind and didn't allow him to get much sleep. When he got up in the morning, he knew he had to figure out a concrete way of realizing it, a means of passing on his wisdom to others. It was on that day that he made his momentous decision, and began to sketch out the philosophical treatise that he would eventually entitle *The Positive Life*. He was fully confident that one day, there would be a plaque posted where the pet-supply factory once stood, announcing that this was the place where the idea for *The Positive Life* first struggled into existence, after a hard day's labor.

Chapter 3.

Museum Visit

When it came to keeping his living space clean and well-organized, Eric Freeman failed to distinguish himself. In short, he was a pig, and he knew it. It bothered him a little – but only a little – that he couldn't keep the apartment clean, but that concern was based on the fact that people – not just friends and relatives, but representatives of the property management company – would sometimes visit him. He personally didn't mind living in a messy environment; it made him feel more comfortable and welcome, every pile or half-empty glass or random sock marking this rented space as his, like a dog pissing to mark territory around the neighborhood. To avoid embarrassment and keep the landlord happy, he sometimes did a general cleanup around the place; but within a few days, it was always back to the usual mess. His new commute out to the suburbs had disrupted even this small habit, by depriving him of an extra hour each day that could be spent on such minor maintenance projects.

It was Sunday evening, and that melancholy feeling, that sense of having entered the last few hours before having to start the work week, was hanging heavily in the apartment. Eric, seeking to dispel this unpleasant mood, decided to start the week early with a writing exercise, perhaps something that he could eventually incorporate into the curriculum he was working on. He rummaged around in the piles of paper on the coffee table in front of him, picking up a small notebook that had a few remaining usable pages. Then he picked up a pen and lay down on the sofa. The exercise for this gloomy evening was to think of his apartment as a Museum of Himself. Writing a prospectus of the museum would enable him to introduce many domestic items in a creative way, which students could then reproduce in their own exercises, thereby cementing their own knowledge. In this spirit, the prospectus for a tour of Eric's Museum of Himself might include descriptions like these:

"The Sock Drawer is one of the highlights of the tour. All of Eric's socks, going back for ten or even more years, are on display here. There are athletic socks that haven't been washed since his college days; you can look at them but touching is not recommended. This is where Eric spends several minutes each day trying to find a matching pair of socks. All the socks are jumbled together, so he has to do this every morning. It says something not good about him that he doesn't take the simple step to sort out his socks. It's a small job that won't take much time, yet he won't do it. Every morning, he wastes several minutes, matching one brown sock with another, or finding an appropriate black mate for a black sock. There are also some socks that have no match, yet he still hasn't thrown them out or repurposed them as cleaning rags, even though they might have been there for years.

"If you're interested in knowing about Eric's approach to hygiene, we recommend the Kitchen Tour. Since he lives in a slovenly bachelor apartment, he has no dishwasher, and has to do the dishes himself. This leads to some hilarious yet disgusting situations, where for example he might be eating breakfast out of the same bowl three days in a row without washing it properly. Eric's so negligent that he thinks a dish is clean if a dog licked it out, just because it now looks clean and shiny! Lucky for him – and for any guests! – that they don't allow dogs in his building.

"The Living Room is where most of Eric's non-work life takes place. There is a TV, but he uses it mainly to watch videos of classic, respectable, and not so respectable movies. He put a lot more money into the stereo system, over there by the wall, with its so-called bookshelf speakers artfully placed on top of, you guessed it, actual bookshelves. The Rega Planar 2 turntable, manufactured during the dark age of vinyl in the late 1980s, was acquired by Eric second-hand, rescued from the unforgiving hands of a collector who was going digital-mad like the rest of society, and who was preparing to toss the thing out. Some people push away thoughts of prospective job loss, pet death, or relationship collapse; in similar fashion, Eric suppresses any fears that his turntable will stop working. The books on his shelves are arranged haphazardly, and represent several different periods of reading, one on top of another, like geological strata. The Living Room Tour examines these strata in some detail, but if you're a casual visitor, all you need to know is that it's a mess of leftover college textbooks inter-spersed with some literary classics; some modern novels and poetry thrown together with no attempt at organi-zation; and random works of non-fiction and reference. A person who didn't like to read might consider the content intimidating; a person who did like to read might wonder why he didn't organize everything better."

31

He was on the verge of writing down this fantasy museum guide when the phone rang. It was his mother. "Is it snowing there?" she asked.

"Yes," said Eric. "Well, it was, until this morning." His mother's calls, while still fairly regular, had become more generic in nature. Eric imagined that she had created a standard checklist for these calls, and was ticking off questions related to health, work, and the weather, one by one. She had moved to Colorado a couple of years before, after his father's death and her own remarriage to a guy named Roger, whom Eric had only met a couple of times. He rarely saw her; the only close relative who remained in the Chicago area was sister Nora, out in Glenview. Their phone talks increasingly sounded like a nurse checking up on a patient.

"It sounds like they moved your company?" Obviously a new piece of information had reached her. "Are you okay with the commute?"

Eric almost said "no," but he didn't want to give her anything to worry about. "It has some positive aspects. I can read on the train. Sometimes I meet someone interesting that I can talk to." This last sentence was a lie.

"I'm glad to hear it."

When he first heard her voice, he thought it would cheer him up at least a little. By the end of the call, he only felt more melancholic. Worse, the phone call had shattered his concentration, and he had lost the urge to write about the Museum of Himself. The melancholy was beginning to verge on a sense of emptiness, something he found more disturbing. Melancholy was a feeling, while the sense of emptiness, the Void, was anti-feeling, like the hum of white noise or an endless gray sky. He decided to go to bed early – the only way he could think of to ward off this fear of the Void.

•

32

Evan Jarrett looked out of his fourth-floor window and into the street, on a day of warming temperatures and melting snow. The weather god of Chicago was asserting his power, showing that he could wipe away the old state of things without asking anyone's permission or giving any warning. Spring was here, and the memory of winter was fading away, at least until the weather god changed his mind again.

A few minutes later, Evan was walking through those streets, on the way to the office of ExactoTemps, on Broadway. His present temp agency was failing to come up with decent jobs, and seeking something a little more secure and lucrative than the improvised handyman jobs that he had been doing to support himself, Evan had submitted an application to this new agency, ExactoTemps, a few weeks previously. Today, they wanted to talk to him. The shining sun and the gurgling rush of meltwater gave him an extra dose of energy, a shot of hope for the future.

When he opened the door to the office of ExactoTemps, his hope cooled just a bit. It was a small office, and most of the available chairs were occupied by people just like him – young, displaced suburbanites who were finding the big city more expensive than they expected, or who had recently lost their jobs. These people were now the competition. He got a cup of coffee and waited to be called; while waiting, he struck up a conversation with the young woman sitting next to him.

"I've been working part-time in an art gallery, but that's not enough to pay the rent," she said. "That's why I'm here. How about you?"

"Well, I'm trying to, uh, launch myself as an entrepreneur, and I've got some seed capital already, but I need to accumulate a little more…" Evan said this with some uncertainty, because he didn't really want to tell her he was a philosopher conducting an experiment in living, or that the "seed capital" he referred to was actually a bribe by his parents to get him to move out of the house. He didn't feel like going into the subject in detail.

Luckily, she didn't ask what kind of entrepreneur he was, since he didn't yet have a convincing answer. "This is a new agency," she informed him. "Just opened in the neighborhood. I think it's worth signing up. I've heard good things about them."

Evan heard his name called, and made his way to the office. Ramona Macquarrie rose to shake his hand. She was a youngish African-American woman of medium height and medium weight, with big glasses and an immaculately pressed sky-blue pantsuit. Evan thought she looked very neat and pristine, which made sense, given that she was new to the job and the agency was new to the neighborhood. "Nice to meet you, Evan. I'm Ramona, the office manager. Thanks for coming in." She began to dig through her file, looking for his application. "Tell me a little about yourself. What sort of positions are you looking for?"

"Any position that will have me," was the first thing that came to Evan's mind. Instead of that he said, "Office jobs mainly. But I'm willing to look at anything."

Ramona frowned as she looked at the application. They talked about willingness to work odd hours, the geographical scope of the jobs, his lack of a car, and his previous experience. "I see you haven't finished college. That could limit your opportunities."

"I've heard that many times before, most recently from my dad," said Evan, trying to be jocular. "My goal is to make enough money to go back to college and finish." This was a lie, but it was a good and useful lie.

"That sounds good, Evan," said Ramona with a smile. "I'd like to give you a short skills test, then we'll have a brief interview. Also, we'll need a urine sample from you."

"That sounds like a lot of fun," said Evan. "Especially the urine sample."

"Oh yeah," said Ramona brightly. "I'm sure that's just what you wanted to do this morning!" Evan was pleased at her response. His goal was to establish a rapport with her, so that she would remember him when giving out the jobs. After a little more calculated joking – Evan didn't want to push his luck – he took the skills test (pretty basic), and did the other required things.

A short time later, Evan emerged from ExactoTemps. She'd call him if anything suitable came up.

Chapter 4.

The Great Displacement

When Eldritch EduWare was acquired by Furuhashi Multimedia Concern, the management of Furuhashi took a look around Eldritch's rather cramped and expensive downtown office and concluded: If we're going to be in America, we might as well have lots of space, as well as easy access to shopping malls, big houses, and cheap golf courses. The decision was quickly made to move Eldritch out of the city, specifically, to the sprawling exurb of Hickory Fields, which was located to the northwest of the city, and which was distinguished by neither hickory nor fields. Thus, at the beginning of the year, Eric Freeman and other diehard urbanites began to make "The Great Displacement," his term for the lengthy daily commute from the city out to Eldritch headquarters. Those compliant souls who had bothered to move out to the suburbs only had to make the

Displacement once; the city dwellers were condemned to do it day after day.

There was an irony to all this, which soon became evident. The upper management in Tokyo, despite their wish to take advantage of American space, sprawl and low real estate costs, wound up treating Eldritch like an absentee landlord. Visits from the higher-ups were rare; they preferred to leave the company's day-to-day functioning in the hands of locally sourced managers. As a result, Eldritch became a fiefdom unto itself, lackadaisically drifting into the future without much input from above. It was a bit like buying a house with an old shed on the edge of the extensive back yard, a shed which you intended to refurbish, but then gradually forgot about. This gradual negligence came as something of a relief to Eric. Since he had lived in Japan for a few months, and had studied the language, some people proposed him as a "liaison officer" or even an interpreter for any Japanese managers that chose to settle and work at Eldritch. In fact, Eric was aware that his own understanding of Japan and its culture was superficial, in a manner characteristic of many liberal-arts college graduates who had stumbled into a major rather than choosing it because they had a real interest in it. Eric could give a PowerPoint presentation on certain aspects of Japanese business practice, and he had a lively appreciation for Japanese New Wave cinema. But his knowledge of the language was mostly degraded beyond use, and the idea of him translating for some of the higher-ups, even in the most casual of settings, was too grotesque even to think about.

Notwithstanding all these considerations, Furuhashi's takeover had inspired Eric to get out his old one-word-a-day Japanese calendar – a learning tool he had used in college – and place it on the nightstand next to his bed. Even though the days and dates didn't match up, the words still had the same meanings. The word for today was *utsukushii* ("beautiful"). Having to get up at six-thirty in the cold and dark didn't feel very *utsukushii* to Eric. When the alarm went off, he forced himself up with the thought that spring was just around the corner and things were bound to get easier. He had time for a quick bowl of cereal and one cup of coffee before he went on his way. He shoved his tie into his jacket pocket; he was going to put it on during the train ride.

The length and complexity of the commute made everything worse. Before the Displacement took effect, he usually took the express bus down Lake Shore Drive, and then walked for about ten minutes. If for some reason he missed the express bus, the El remained an option. Now, he still took the bus or the El – but instead of a short walk, he then had to catch a Metra train, the line going out to the northwest suburbs. Unless he was able to hitch a ride with someone, he had to do the Displacement again in reverse on the way back. Overall, the Great Displacement added almost ten hours a week to his commute: a large chunk of time that he wished he could devote to something else. He was beginning to notice a gradual wearying effect – a feeling of accumulated fatigue, which usually hit him during the afternoon on Thursday, or even on Wednesday night. He had never had to deal with this before. Previously he had enjoyed going out on Friday night, but now he preferred to huddle in his apartment, a human battery recharging itself. To gain more freedom and cut the commuting time, he had begun to toy with the idea of buying a car, but doubted that he could justify the hefty additional expense under his current circumstances. The other option – moving out to the suburbs to be closer to the job – did not appeal to him at all, but he couldn't rule it out. The new commute did have one positive aspect: it provided a lot of time for reading things he might not have gotten around to under less confined circumstances.

One thing which pleased him about the commute was that the train was only about half full. The usual flow of traffic this time of day was into the city, and those trains must have been packed with besuited suburbanites poring over their business and sports news, management books, suspense novels, crossword puzzles, and horoscopes. Eric made himself comfortable at a seat on the upper deck of the car, which afforded him a better view. His reading material for this trip was *Revolutionary Road* by Richard Yates, the classic novel of death and disillusionment in the suburbs. Eric had started reading the novel some time before, then set it aside. The combination of the Great Displacement, with its associated daily trip to the suburbs, and his recent encounters with Porter and Nora Hotchkiss had induced him to pick it up again. Now, when reading it, he was comparing the main characters – a married couple who were residents of a Connecticut suburb of New York City in the 1950s – with Nora and Porter. The distance between the two couples was considerable. Eric had to laugh (not too loudly, so as not to disturb the other commuters) when he read that Frank Wheeler, Yates' hero, considered himself to be "an intense, nicotine-stained, Jean-Paul-Sartre sort of man." By contrast, Porter was dead set against smoking, which he regarded puritanically as a great and lower-class evil, and almost certainly he had no idea who Jean-Paul Sartre was. But what was the more important difference here, Eric asked himself: the one between the real Porter Hotchkiss and the fictional Frank Wheeler, or the one between the 1950s and the 1990s? What fun it must have been to proclaim yourself an "existentialist," holding forth about the meaning of life while smoking hand-rolled cigarettes, sporting a black beret, and spinning Miles Davis records. Richard Yates had meant his book to be a critique of the suffocating conformity of the 1950s, but in Eric's view, today's upper-middle-class, upwardly mobile families made the conformists of *Revolutionary Road* – whatever their faults may have been – look like bold individualists.

Mild morning light was bathing the scene as the train pulled out of Union Station. Well-dressed people were walking the streets, taxis were whizzing about. Slickly decorated restaurants and stores lying the cityscape. But this scene vanished as the train groaned its way northwest like a slow-moving animal; it was soon traversing an eerie industrial landscape of enormous buildings and outdoor storage lots piled high with all manner of products and various junk. One of Eric's favorite sights on the trip was a vast automobile graveyard. It stretched on and on, for blocks or maybe even a mile or two, looking like the most apocalyptic highway pileup in the history of the world. He wouldn't have been surprised to see mangled human and animal bodies lying here and there, but the only corpses on display were of the automotive kind.

Eventually, this landscape gave way to a classic tableau of urban America as the train began to plow its way through the Northwest Side. Rows and rows of bungalows alternated with factories, warehouses, and lots both vacant and full. Individual enterprise was still obvious out here: Harvey's Diner, Fred's Bar, Miguel's Hardware. Signs were in Spanish, Polish, Korean, and sometimes English. You could bet these were real people, too: Harvey with his thinning gray hair, cigar and heavy black-rimmed glasses; Fred with his combover, mustache and paunch; Miguel with his full head of black hair, aviator sunglasses, and toothy smile. Recent immigrants jostled with long-entrenched working-class communities for control of the streets. There were new people, from different parts of the world, walking those streets now, but from the train window, things seemed to have barely changed in the last thirty or more years. Fine dining wasn't an option around here, to judge by the proliferation of burger joints and donut shops (not shoppes).

It wasn't easy to tell where the city ended and the suburbs began. The Western suburbs immediately outside the city were really just a continuation of the urban industrial belt. Maybe the streets were a bit wider, but the general appearance was the same. After a while Eric noticed the newness of construction – boxy buildings from the post-1945 era, dull and lacking in any character or distinction. The farther out the train went, the greater the proliferation of twisting dead-end streets, shopping malls with enormous parking lots, tiny forlorn business districts, houses identical in construction and differing only in color, office parks, and huddled houses of the same type, apparently meant to form some kind of "community."

The continuity was broken by a strip of forest preserve as the train entered the home stretch. When the trees cleared, it was as if the whole scene had been doused in some sort of antiseptic. Everything was clean and scrubbed, and the sense of space, of arriving in a vast flat region that stretched for thousands of miles, was startling after the urban crush. There were no broken windows, graffiti or litter. There were also no sidewalks, no pedestrians, no mom-and-pop stores, no restaurants that were not part of a chain, no entertainment venues outside of a shopping mall, no downtown to speak of, no public parks of any size, no buildings of any architectural distinction whatsoever – nothing to attract or disturb the eye with any sense of spontaneity or individuality.

Eric used a simple classification system regarding the suburbs – there were good ones and bad ones. The good ones boasted houses designed by Frank Lloyd Wright or some other distinguished architect, a wide range of cultural events, or extensive green spaces by the lakefront. The bad ones were places like Hickory Fields. The basic building unit of the bad suburbs was the box. Boxes of various sizes and colors, of concrete, glass, steel and brick, big and small

41

boxes arranged upright and sideways, black, white, gray, brown and transparent boxes, boxes stuck together like Legos or separated by swathes of asphalt, boxes with yards of grass or yards of concrete, could be seen everywhere as you looked out the train window.

Strip malls, mini-malls, and shopping centers alternated with identikit housing developments that bore fanciful names, like Avalon Estates, Balmoral-on-the-Lake, Provence-in-the-Woods, and Renaissance Acres: names that inadvertently highlighted their aesthetic failings. Criss-crossing this townscape were the gray ribbons of streets and highways, which met each other at odd angles and groaned under streams of traffic moving in irregular jolts and lurches. As the train started to slow down, Eric thought, Welcome to the exurbs! It's progress! It's the way we live now! And it's the way we're going to live until the oil runs out or the sun explodes, at which point the entire world will look like the great West Side automobile graveyard.

The Metra station where Eric got off was planted with signs displaying the official name of the suburb, which was Hickory Fields. However, he had already decided to rename the town Boxville in his own mind. It was his own little truth-in-advertising campaign; as was the case with the name "Greenland," calling this place Hickory Fields represented a deliberate attempt to mislead and entice potential settlers. He arrived at the Boxville station, which was basically all platform with only a couple of cold-weather shelters, and from it, Eric saw the three-story gunmetal-gray box occupied by Eldritch, shining in the morning light. He made his way along the grassy side of a major road (no sidewalk, of course), past an auto-parts store and a diner, and then through Eldritch's parking lot, into which cars were turning. Up the stairs he went; the door opened; and then he was out of the cold, in a familiar world of coffee smells and ringing phones, with the smile of the receptionist, Lydia Walters, to greet him. "Hey Liddy," he said.

"Hey Eric. Didja have a nice weekend?" Lydia's Southwest Side accent had survived the Great Displacement intact.

"I sure did." He was going to ask her the same question, but her phone rang, so he just smiled, waved goodbye, and headed down the left passage from the front desk, then up to the second floor, where his cubicle was located. It was time for the Routine: first the coffee, then the booting-up of the computer, the checking of e-mail and of phone messages. While pouring himself some coffee, he wondered if he could eventually get a dispensation from the management allowing him to work at home at least some of the time. Only two months of commuting, and already he was sick of it.

Eric's cubicle was one of many occupying a spacious floor. The dominant colors were blue and green, meant to produce a relaxing atmosphere, which was somewhat compromised by the fluorescent lights overhead and the glare from outside, a product of the glint of the sun bouncing off the cars in the parking lot. The latter could get particularly fierce on sunny days, so Eric kept a pair of sunglasses in his desk to cut the annoyance. He had to be stingy about wearing them around the office, though: some of the higher-ups seemed to think he was trying to be a "cool cat" and diluting the solemn corporate atmosphere they were at pains to cultivate. Eric was lucky in one respect. His cubicle was in the corner. This meant that people never came his way unless they were looking specifically for him. Since he didn't have a constant stream of human traffic going by, he had no particular reason to look busy. Also, he was able to tell by looking at the reflection in the window if anyone was coming. If so, he had approximately four seconds to get his feet off the desk, close whatever book or magazine he was reading, and look busy and serious about work. If it was

Woody Latour, the head of the department, he had more like ten seconds, since Woody lumbered quite a bit.

A few people were at their workstations, sitting in the quietude of early morning catatonia. Eric waved weakly to them, or said "hi" very softly. He turned to the left and was confronted by the sight of Mike Riordan, his colleague in the Curriculum Development department, who acknowledged him by raising his head from a piece of paper and mumbling. Mike was about forty, thin and bespectacled, generally pretty quiet, and often made Eric nervous because he usually seemed to be worried about something. Eric went through the computer part of the Routine (no surprises in his inbox), and was relaxing with the coffee when Mike padded softly over, holding a couple of large envelopes in his hand.

"More?" asked Eric.

"Yep."

Mike dropped the envelopes on Eric's desk. Recently, Eldritch had placed an ad in the *Chronicle of Higher Education* soliciting freelance writers to help in its latest educational project, which involved creating English-language teaching content for international markets. So dry was the academic job market that Eric and Mike had been swamped by grad students and other campus denizens looking for some way to use their skills.

Another desperate would-be academic trying to keep from starving, thought Eric as he opened the first application. There were the usual papers: resume, letters of recommendation testifying that Sanjay Kumar was the greatest person to walk the earth since Jesus Christ, Confucius, and Gautama the Buddha, and writing samples. There was also a CD. The words "Introducing Sanjay" were printed on it. Good God, the things people did to get even part-time work!

Dreading what he might find, Eric put the CD into the computer. Instantly a wave of techno-pop dance-type music started to pulse out of the speakers, and a voice said "Welcome to the world of Sanjay!"

"What are you listening to over there?" said Mike from the next cubicle.

"Oh, another job applicant has gone above and beyond the call of duty," said Eric. The smiling face of Sanjay appeared briefly on the screen; then it and the music both faded, and a different earnest young man came on. "I've known Sanjay for twelve years now," this fellow said, "and during this time, I can honestly say that I've never met anyone else who has such a range of talents..."

Eric watched this presentation with a sort of bemused horror. Sanjay Kumar was obviously yet another product of the insanely competitive world of the rich suburbs, the kind of environment where every other car sport-ed a rear-window sticker with "Harvard" or "Penn" or "Northwestern" on it, testimony to the success of sta-tus-obsessed parents. It was a milieu that Eric knew well. Sanjay was probably spending his twenties in the pursuit of two or even three degrees, racking up huge debts so he could join the elite; cohabitating with a wom-an (or man) who was doing the same thing; and asking himself with every step he took, How will this add to my marketability?

A still photo of Sanjay holding a volleyball and laugh-ing was gradually covered up by a scrolling list of his accomplishments. Had a play produced at the Pennsylva-nia Youth Arts Festival; was an intern at the Brookings Institution; mentored at-risk youth in deprived neigh-borhoods of Philadelphia; plays the clarinet –

"I love that term 'at-risk youth'," said Eric to no one in particular. "In reality, it's not the youth that are at risk; it's the people around them."

"So our friend Sanjay has a social conscience on the side?" said Mike.

45

"Looks like it," said Eric. "Maybe he should stick with that, it probably pays more than we do." Sanjay himself returned to the screen. This time, he was in a classroom, wearing a serious look on his face, holding a sheaf of papers and apparently giving a lecture of some kind. Peaceful music (flute and guitar) emanated from the speakers. There may have been some at-risk youth in the room, but if so they were not shown. Sanjay himself intoned: "We all know the proverb about giving a man a fish..."

"You know what's wrong with these people?" said Eric.

"What people?" shouted Mike from twelve feet away.

"People like Sanjay. Their problem is that from day one, they've been told how special they are. Their parents say: 'Sanjay, or Taylor, or Tiffany, or whatever your name is, you are a unique and wonderful human being.' And these kids grow up believing it. What they really need is someone to tell them they're pretty much interchangeable with thousands of other people."

"The truth is hard to take," said Mike.

Eric decided to shut off *The Sanjay Kumar Show* and look at somebody else. Strange, in this "boom economy," that so many intelligent people were desperate for jobs. The next application was a case in point. It came from a Dr. Paul Frumkin, who claimed to be a philosophy professor at Eastbrook College, a respectable institution located in rural Wisconsin. Apparently the threadbare academic life was starting to wear on Dr. Frumkin. Whether the problem was the lack of money, the lack of recognition, the onerous teaching duties, the onerous publication duties, the small-town dullness where the only thing you can feel is yourself getting older (while your students remain eternally young), or a combination of these things, Eric didn't know; but he knew the basic ingredients that went into the mix.

Frumkin's resume caught Eric's eye immediately. At the top, above the usual contact information, was a quote from Pascal: "The eternal silence of these infinite spaces terrifies me." Me too, thought Eric, before he registered just how strange this looked in context.

All of these applicants portrayed themselves as extraordinary people, yet they seemed desperate to escape whatever situation they found themselves in. Eric took a couple of minutes to review some of the choicer specimens. There was Kathy M., who was writing a thesis on "mountaintop removal and its economic consequences" at some university in West Virginia. There was John McG., who had just completed a novel about the coming-of-age of a sensitive gay Cherokee Indian. There was Ellen W., who had not one but *two* PhD.'s and still couldn't find a permanent university job, despite the fact that she played the oboe and had written an article on the novels of Knut Hamsun, in Norwegian no less. There was Michael A., whose specialty was teaching writing skills to functional illiterates ("being a dyslexic, I understand some of the issues these people face"). There was Linda O., whose six-page resume listed every poem she had ever published in every obscure literary mag, including "Thoughts on the Children's Ward at the Roanoke City Hospital" (in *Rappahannock Quarterly*) and "To My Father Dying of Alzheimer's" (in *Grit: The Literary Magazine of The Colorado School of Mines*). There was Aldritch J., who seemed to think that the similarity of his name to that of the company that had placed the ad was an omen of their eventual collaboration. There was Tupac X (his last name, not an initial), who was a longtime member of the Nation of Islam and was volunteering his services as a "sensitivity consultant" should Eldritch wish to market its goods in Islamic countries. There was Juan F., who mentored at-risk youth in Philadelphia ("Hey, I bet he knows Sanjay," thought Eric). There was Roofus B., who claimed that he had developed his writing skills "as a way of dealing with my anger management issues." There was Emily E., a poet who included a reference written for her by another poet (a fairly well-known figure in the poetic world), who had described Emily as "one of the most outstanding poets of her young generation... a brilliant soul, whose creativity – so on the verge of a grand eruption, a leap into a new, radiant mode of expressivity – would particularly benefit from the security that steady work would give her." And there was Gerald C., who lived in Australia, and had apparently responded to the wrong ad ("I am a hydraulic engineer of over twenty years' experience").

But only Paul F. had the guts to put a quotation from a philosopher at the top of his resume, and not an optimistic, life-affirming quotation, but an expression of cosmic despair. Just for this, Eric liked Paul already. *Utsukushii*, Professor, he thought. The positive first impression was confirmed by the professor's letter.

Dear Mr. Freeman:

I'm responding to your ad in The Chronicle of Higher Education. My work record speaks for itself, so I'm not going to deal with that here. The fact is, I can think of a lot of things I'd rather do than create content for teaching the language of Shakespeare and Elvis Presley to people who aren't lucky enough to speak it already. But as a philosopher I know we have to face reality sooner or later, and anything which helps us do that, like the little bit of extra money I expect to make from collaborating with you, is good.

You see, Mr. Freeman, I'm an expert in German philosophy of the nineteenth century. This is not simple stuff, and I've put a lot of effort into understanding it. But when I mention names like Hegel, Schopenhauer, and Nietzsche to people around here, they think I'm referring to one of the local microbreweries, or maybe the quarterback for the college football team. Even after

the students find out more about these guys, they don't care.
I'm forty-eight years old, and lately I've been thinking about
chucking the college gig altogether.

Two more paragraphs in the same vein followed. Upon
reaching the end, Eric sat motionless for a couple of minutes, then rose and walked to Mike Riordan's cubicle.

Mike was in the process of hanging up his phone. He
turned around and saw Eric standing there. "What's up?"

"You know this freelance business?" said Eric. "I was
wondering how much leeway I have to deal with these
people."

"You mean the writers?"

"Yes. Like, do I have permission to decide who to work
with, and under what circumstances, and so forth?"

"Absolutely," said Mike firmly. "In fact I'd be glad to
leave that project entirely under your supervision, if you
want it that way. I'm going to have my hands full with
this software thing for a while."

"Okay. So I can go ahead and hire people."

"Got some good ones?"

"I think so," said Eric, walking back to his desk. "We'll
see."

Mike's phone rang again. A laconic conversation en-
sued. It was clear that whoever was calling wanted to
see him in person. He hung up and walked away. Eric
watched him go, then sat down, located Frumkin's phone
number, and dialed.

"Hello?" came a somewhat muffled voice.

"Hi, I'd like to speak to Dr. Frumkin, please."

"You got him." He sounded tired. "What can I do for
you?"

Eric introduced himself. Frumkin seemed to perk up
a little. "Oh yeah? You actually liked my application?
Whaddaya know."

"Yes indeed. It stood out. It's rare to see such honesty from a job seeker."

"Wow, that's great." Eric heard a springy noise in the background, as if Dr. Frumkin were forcing himself out of bed. "Maybe honesty really is the best policy."

"Maybe so," mumbled Eric.

"So, whaddaya think? Can you guys use me?"

"Quite possibly. Right now, I'm in the process of putting a team together. I'd like to send you, oh, maybe a small assignment, and take things from there. How does that sound?"

"That sounds just great," said Frumkin. "Hey listen, can we work out the details later? I gotta go to my phenomenology class in a few minutes."

"Wouldn't you rather relax on the porch with a can of Schopenhauer's?" asked Eric.

Frumkin laughed. "Hey, yeah, wouldn't we all."

Eric pushed himself up from his chair to make sure that Mike was still out of earshot. "You know what, Paul? I'd like to join you on that porch. I don't like my job any more than you do yours. But I'm too lazy and unmotivated to look for a new one. That's not the whole explanation, though. Any new job I take will probably turn out to be just as bad as the one I've got now. I'm starting to find out that's just the way life is. I wouldn't have thought this ten or even five years ago. But now I don't think it, I know it in my bones. I can tell from your letter that when you started teaching at that college of yours, you were bright and optimistic and liked what you were doing. You thought it was important. You don't think that anymore. Am I right?"

There was a pause while a sound like leaking air emerged from the phone; then Frumkin let out a laugh. "Hey, you nailed me. But I still gotta eat. We'll talk later, okay?"

"Okay."

Just as Eric hung up, he looked over the cubicle wall and saw Mike walking in his direction. "You got any appointments this afternoon?" asked Mike.

"No. Why?"

"Woody wants to meet with us about three o'clock. Second floor conference room."

"Fine. I can do that."

Woody Latour was the head of the Curriculum Development department. On paper, he looked like a great choice for that position. He had an Oxford Ph.D. (or D.Phil., as that university eccentrically called it), had gone to a fancy boarding school on the East Coast, and possessed extensive teaching experience at the high school and university level. But one thing that made him stand out, and that had won over the management when they were hiring for this job, was his gift as a raconteur and public speaker. Woody's talent at entertaining, amusing, and cajoling audiences made him invaluable when speaking at seminars and conventions. When he was enthusiastic about something, he could be mesmerizing, even if his listeners had a hard time remembering what he had said afterwards. Outsiders and managers got the impression that the Curriculum Development department was a dynamic place under Woody Latour's leadership.

That had been the case for a while, anyway. After he'd been in the job for a couple of years, a notable sloppiness began to creep into Woody's personal habits, and then into his work performance. Woody was no stranger to the pleasures of the table, and consequently he had long had trouble keeping his weight under control. In his new position, with more money at his disposal and the associated perks and benefits, he had allowed himself to balloon to almost spherical dimensions by taking advantage of the endless helpings of food available at conventions, business lunches and dinners, and various other catered events. The constant use of taxis and chauffeurs, subsidized by the company, meant that he got no exercise, thereby putting further strain on his health. At the same time, his absences from the workplace had become more frequent and inexplicable. He could get away with this because upper management rarely took an interest in the day-to-day doings of Curriculum Development. And since the Great Displacement had gone into effect, when he did show up for work, he had developed a habit of taking naps at his desk after lunch. Only a handful of people were aware of these aspects of Woody's behavior. Mike Riordan, who sometimes had occasion to go to Woody's office, had interrupted him once or twice in the middle of a snooze. Woody, upon finding his wits, had described this as a form of "postprandial meditation," something that helped him concentrate on the challenging intellectual tasks ahead. Mike did not tell anyone other than Eric of Woody's naps or absences; he kept these things to himself, in case such knowledge should ever turn out to be useful.

Chapter 5.

Phoning It In

The weather was now consistently warmer and sunnier, and Evan Jarrett concluded that it was time to put his snow shovel into storage and look for some other way of supporting himself. He called his original temp agency, the one that had gotten him such memorable gigs as the pet-supply job, but they had nothing suitable at the moment. He received a more positive response from the firm he had just signed up with, ExactoTemps.

"I've only got one thing right now, Evan," said Ramona Macquarrie over the phone. "It involves a lot of phone work. Can you handle that?"

"What is it exactly?"

"It's not telemarketing, but you will be calling people. It's phone surveying. You call up a lot of people, and they answer a questionnaire."

"So it's like polling?"

"A little. All you do is ask them questions and write down the answers. You're not selling them anything."

"That's good. Questions about what?"

"Travel. How often they do it, how much money they spend, where they go. How does that sound?"

Evan wasn't crazy about the idea of making hundreds of calls to complete strangers, but his finances were shaky at the moment, and he didn't feel confident about holding out for anything better. "Okay, I'll take it."

Ramona gave him the details: a five-day job, twelve noon to eight o'clock at night, taking place downtown on the premises of a large insurance company, starting the next day. But first, he had to attend a two-hour preliminary meeting with his temp colleagues and the supervisor of the project, to be held starting at four o'clock that very day.

And thus, a few hours after his chat with Ramona, Evan Jarrett entered an office tower located in the grid-like, cavernous environs of Union Station. He made his way to a large room, empty except for several desks and chairs. His steps were muffled by thick beige carpeting as he entered. Blinds were drawn over the windows, blocking any view outside. A couple of temps were already seated at their desks when he arrived; they were chatting to each other about their last assignment.

"I like accounts receivable," said one of them, a pudgy, bespectacled man of about forty. "Doris was always nice. As long as I got my quota done by the end of the day, she didn't hassle me."

"Yeah, well you should be glad you didn't have to deal with that scumbag Schultz," said the other, a blonde girl who wore a lot of rings and was twisting her hair around her finger. "What an arrogant bastard."

Their names were Edgar and Tracy, as Evan found out when he introduced himself. Edgar had lost his job the previous year, and had been temping ever since. Tracy was trying to raise money to attend beauty school. Evan decided not to tell them he was a philosopher; he wasn't in the mood to answer hostile questions. He said he was a student trying to make some money on the side.

Three more temps entered and took their seats, and right behind them came Mr. Brendan Frost, the supervisor of this project. He was a stiff, middle-aged, mustachioed man of medium height with slick iron-gray hair, attired in a blue suit. His gaze was steely and his movements jerky and impulsive; he reminded Evan of a highly energetic robot. With all the temps at their desks and focusing on him, he introduced himself, then asked the temps to say their names. Mr. Frost worked for a large market research firm; this phone survey project had been commissioned by the insurance company. "You have a list of people, with their phone numbers, on your desks. You also have a stack of questionnaires. You'll be calling up these people, asking them questions, and writing down the answers. Any questions?"

One of the temps raised his hand. "Who are these people?"

"Who are these people?" repeated Mr. Frost. "Answer: they're just ordinary people, selected at random throughout the metropolitan area. Now, there are always problems with that. Some of the people will be uncooperative. Some may even be hostile. Some may be difficult to deal with. Some of them won't be able to speak English."

"Then why are we calling them?" asked Tracy. The others chuckled.

Mr. Frost said: "These lists are generated by computer. They can't determine the language skills of the people you are calling. If you get a person who doesn't speak English, say 'I'm sorry,' hang up, and go on to the next number on the list."

Mr. Frost continued, laying out the procedure for them, and warning them that he would be able to listen in on their calls via the phone on his desk, so "Don't try any funny business." Just before the meeting ended, he gave them instructions for a special project he wanted them to do at home, before they came to work for the first day of calling.

"I'd like you all to make a call register," he said. "What do I mean by a call register? Answer: I mean you take a piece of paper, make a list of the names and numbers of people you're calling, and leave space next to their names. Then you're going to put three boxes next to each name: completed survey, declined to take survey, did not qualify, and did not answer phone. Did I say three boxes? I meant four. And did I say write down the names? You don't have to do that till you get here and start calling. Just create the three boxes, sorry, four boxes, and write the names and numbers as you call them. Anyway, please do at least one page like this before you show up tomorrow. It will save valuable time." He ended this speech with a sudden karate-chop gesture toward his audience. "Any questions?"

"Yeah," said Edgar. "How long should we take to make this call register?"

"It shouldn't take more than about fifteen minutes. You can do it at home, or you can come here early and do it."

"Excuse me," said Evan. "Are we getting paid for this?"

"Are you getting paid?" Mr. Frost said this in a disbelieving tone of voice, as if he thought Evan was stupid. A couple of the temps laughed.

"I don't mean for the job," said Evan. "I mean for the time it takes to make the call register."

Mr. Frost frowned. "But Evan – your name is Evan, right? This is only fifteen extra minutes a day."

"Yes, but there's a principle involved. If we work, we should get paid."

Mr. Frost looked stumped, but he recovered quickly. "How do you get here, Evan?"

"What do you mean?"

"Do you drive or take public transport?"

"Public transport."

"Can't you make the call register while you're traveling here?"

"I'm sorry," said Evan forcefully, "but that's still work. We should all get paid for it, even if it's only fifteen extra minutes a day." Murmurs of agreement were heard from some of the other temps.

"Okay," said Mr. Frost, who saw which way the wind was blowing. "I'll let all of you put an extra hour on your timesheets. It's a five-day project, so that should cover it." He decided to wrap things up for the day. Refusing to take any more questions, he dismissed the meeting. "I'll see everyone at noon tomorrow."

When Mr. Frost had left, Edgar came up to Evan. "Thanks for doing that, man."

"It's a matter of principle, you know," said Evan. "I did it, but nothing stops you from doing it yourself."

"Oh, I can't afford to take the risk."

"Yeah, good job, Evan," said Tracy, slinging on her coat. "We appreciate it."

Evan exited the building with the rest of them. The group broke up as the temps went their separate ways, and Evan was left to enjoy the fading sunlight, which struck fiery shards of red and orange off the glass and steel towers around him. A minor triumph, he thought, and all the more admirable because he had put himself at risk. The purity of his own motivations, more than anything else, impressed Evan.

•

Late the next morning, before heading downtown for the first day of calling, Evan went to the supermarket in search of free samples. Usually he could build a modest meal from them: a tiny wedge of pizza, a paper cup of wine, and a bite of sausage didn't add up to much, but it was better than nothing. Today they were promoting cheese. White and orange blocks of it stood wrapped in plastic on a table. There were free samples, too – little chunks on a dish with toothpicks next to them. Evan's stomach groaned at the sight. He grabbed a toothpick and speared a few of the little chunks onto it, then shoved them into his mouth. That took care of lunch.

Evan started phoning at twelve o'clock. He had a list with hundreds of names on it – Garcias, Kellys, Patels, Urbanczyks, Changs, Korolenkos, Taylors, Nguyens, Duponts, Souzas, Murrays, Hovhanissians, and Steinbergs – and didn't like the thought of calling up all these people he didn't know. However, Mr. Frost was sitting behind the temps, observing them from his own desk, and occasionally listening in on their calls, so Evan had no choice. He tried to get through the calls as quickly and efficiently as possible. The questionnaire normally took about ten minutes to get through, and frequently the people he was calling would get impatient. "How much longer is this going to take?" they would ask. "Just a couple of minutes," Evan would tell them, which was what Mr. Frost had told him to say.

Despite his efficient work methods, it didn't take long for Evan to get sick of the job. Most of the people he called were hostile, and the non-hostile ones were lonely and glad of the opportunity to talk to someone. He disliked having to cut short a conversation with a chatty person, because he knew that, statistically speaking, the next person he called was likely to be unfriendly or difficult. Pronouncing some of the names on the list could be a problem. Confronted with "Ms. Gloria Beneke," Evan couldn't decide if he should ask for Ms. *Ben*ekee, Ms. Be*neek*, or Ms. Be*nee*kee. He chose the last one at random.

"This is Gloria *Ben*ekee," was the response, "and I don't want to buy anything." She hung up.

Mr. Elmer Winkelmann, on the other hand, was quite eager to talk. "How many times have you flown in the last year?" Evan asked him.

"I haven't been in an airplane since 1967," he said.

"Thank you, but you do not qualify," said Evan, following the script. As he hung up, he heard Mr. Winkelmann say "Huh?"

Jimmy Lewis was quite skeptical. "A survey? Go ahead, but if this is a sales pitch, I'm gonna be one pissed-off guy."

Evan reassured him. Jimmy answered the first few questions, then grew hostile. "How much longer is this gonna take?"

"Just a couple minutes. Taking all expenses into account, how much did you spend on your last vacation?"

"Who wants to know? What company is behind this survey?"

Evan looked around. Mr. Frost had abandoned his listening post and was walking out of the room. "I can assure you that this survey is not being done by any company, and certainly not by United Insurance International."

Jimmy laughed. "Oh, I get it. You're probably not supposed to say that." Since he appreciated Evan's candor, he finished the survey.

Another respondent said, "That's none of your business," and hung up.

"*No hablo inglés*," said another.

"*Nie rozumiem po angielsku*," said yet another.

"You've reached the Morrison residence," said a machine. "If you'd like to leave a message — "

Some people seemed to regard Evan as a spur to the imagination. Robert O'Rourke was one of them.

"Taking all expenses into account, how much did you spend on your last vacation?" Evan asked him.

"*All* expenses? Why that would amount to, let me see, five hundred million dollars."

"I see," said Evan, who wrote down the figure automatically, without paying attention. "And where did you go?"

"Oh, I went to all kinds of places," said Robert with enthusiasm. "First I visited Rio to see the Carnival. Then I went to the Sahara Desert. That was kind of boring so I left after two days. Nothing to eat, you know, and it gets so damn hot! After that, I made my way to Florida, where I hired a spaceship and went to the moon."

After the comment about the moon, Evan stopped writing things down. At this point he was supposed to hang up on the prankster and go on to the next person. However, he wanted to see what heights of absurdity Robert's story would reach.

"When I got to the moon, I discovered I had made a big mistake: I forgot to bring food and oxygen! Well, there was nothing left to do but go back to Earth. I picked up some oxygen tanks and a few cans of soup, and I was preparing to go back when I thought: Hey, I've already seen the moon, maybe I should go to Mars instead!" Evan heard laughter echoing faintly in the background; apparently this performance was not intended just for him.

"Okay," deadpanned Evan, "did you use a travel agency, or did you make all the arrangements yourself?"

After seven hours of this kind of work, Evan's left ear hurt from listening to the phone, his voice was hoarse from talking, his body was stiff from sitting in the same position all day, and he was ravenously hungry – the free cheese from the supermarket wasn't enough to sustain him. The hostile and uncooperative attitude of so many callers didn't help. But now their work was done, and Mr. Frost came before them to discuss the day's events.

"Okay, first day wasn't bad. Richard, you have a friendly voice, that's good, but don't talk too long to the respondents. Tracy, speak up a little." All the tele-surveyors were tired and sat there meekly while Mr. Frost rattled off a list of comments and corrections. "Edgar, do you have a bladder problem?"

"What?" said Edgar.

"I noticed you went many times to the bathroom," said Mr. Frost. "An average of one point eight times per hour, in fact. So I repeat the question: Do you have a bladder problem?"

"Um, no." Edgar's face was red and his voice was meek.

"Then why," said Mr. Frost, not raising his voice at all, but maintaining vocal coolness, "is it necessary for you to make so many trips to the bathroom?"

Edgar stumbled his way through an answer, saying that talking on the phone dried out his throat, so that he needed water. Everyone else sat there with frozen expressions on their faces, not sure how to react to this, and fearful that they would be picked on next.

"Excuse me, Mr. Frost!" blurted Evan.

"Yes, Evan?" said Mr. Frost, visibly rattled at this interruption.

"If you have a problem with Edgar's behavior, please take it up with him in private. The rest of us don't need to know about it. It's none of our business."

Mr. Frost stared at Evan with a frown, but didn't say anything. The other workers had all turned to look at Evan. They seemed relieved that someone had spoken out. Evan, however, couldn't think what to say next. He sat silently, bit his lip, and fidgeted.

Mr. Frost looked as if he were going to get angry, but the look passed. "You know, Evan, maybe this job is not for you. Not everyone can be a good telephone researcher. It is possible that you do not have the patience and temperament to be good at this."

Evan found his voice again. "The issue isn't whether I'm a good telephone researcher or not. It's whether you have the right to embarrass one of your employees in front of the others."

Mr. Frost clearly wasn't expecting such insubordination. "I can understand that you want to avoid talking about your deficiencies. But if you won't talk about them, we can't correct them."

"But my deficiencies are not the issue," Evan protested. "The issue is how you treated — "

"Why do you think that I'm embarrassing you if I talk about your deficiencies?" said Mr. Frost. His voice sounded just a little hurt.

"But you're not embarrassing *me*, you're embarrassing Edgar."

"By talking about *your* deficiencies, I'm embarrassing Edgar?" said Mr. Frost. He looked genuinely nonplussed. "How do you come to that conclusion?"

Evan stared at him in confusion. Now he was embarrassed, simply because he had allowed his opponent to control the shape of the argument. He had to get back to the fork in the road where the trouble started. "You embarrassed Edgar. Then, you tried to shift the argument to the question of my deficiencies. I was protesting against the fact that you were embarrassing Edgar."

Mr. Frost countered: "You were protesting, because you thought it would be embarrassing to discuss your deficiencies in front of everyone. But we are a group. We treat everyone equally. Why should you get special treatment?"

Evan could think of nothing to say. He looked around the room, scouting for allies. It was in vain. A couple of people were staring at their desks; Tracy was playing with her pen, focusing her attention mightily upon that implement; Richard was looking at Mr. Frost with studious impassivity. Only Edgar was daring to look in Evan's direction:

his head was lowered, but his eyes seemed to say *thanks, buddy*.

It was clear that his triumph of the previous day would not be repeated. Mr. Frost began talking again, at a notably quicker pace, as if he were eager to put this awkward incident behind him. "We are a team. What does it mean to be a team? Answer: it means teamwork is important. You people did pretty well considering it's only your first day. But there's plenty of room for improvement. I expect things to go better tomorrow. In fact, I *insist* on things going better tomorrow. See you then." He waved to them, signaling that it was time for the group to disperse. The temps gathered their things and left in silence.

•

Reflecting on the events of the two days, Evan concluded that they essentially constituted a clash between two *scripts*. Evan had his own script that he followed. One part of Evan's script consisted of workers' rights. This was a matter of law and policy; these things gave him a rock to stand on and a defense against the rhetoric deployed by Brendan Frost. This was the source of his achievement on the first day.

Unfortunately for him, Mr. Frost's script was triumphant on the second day. Evan could convince Frost to pay the temps, but he had not yet figured out a way to alter Frost's personal behavior toward them. Frost was a marketing professional. He had many years of experience deploying rhetoric to get the results he wanted. Evan had no such background and no defense against that type of manipulation.

Evan regarded the chapter of *The Positive Life* that dealt with altruism as one of the most important of the treatise. After his encounter with Brendan Frost, he realized that writing it would be a more difficult task than he initially imagined. He had twice acted altruistically, but the team rallied behind him only once.

The next morning, while Evan was starting the day, Ramona Macquarrie called from ExactoTemps. "Evan, we're taking you off this job. Don't go in to work today."

"Why?"

"The client has decided that the job is not a good fit for you."

"Is that so."

"You'll get paid for the work you did, of course. But Mr. Frost, who is leading the project, said that you are not a team player. He only wants team players on his team, is what he tells me. We have a couple of our other temps on this job, and we have received no complaints about them."

Evan struggled to think of something to say. It was early in the morning, he had just rolled out of bed, and his mind was working slowly. "I'm sorry if I caused any trouble. But if you have other temps on this job, I think you should discuss it with them. The client is being abusive. Ask the temps, and they will confirm it."

"We might do that. It depends on how serious the abuse is. But we still don't want you going in today. You might need to rethink your attitude if you want to continue to get jobs of this kind. Maybe you should think a bit more about precisely what assignments you want. That would help both you and us."

When the call finished, Evan felt relief. Although he was now once again unemployed – only for a short time, he hoped – he was glad to be removed from this job. Mr. Frost was right about at least one thing: he was not a team player.

Chapter 6.

S a b i

Eric Freeman carried a map in his head. It was an interactive map, one that he unfolded on weekends and during other blocks of free time, and its organizing principle was his own personal interest in things. At the center of the map was his apartment. Radiating out from the center were the streets and buildings of his neighborhood, though in a very patchy, sometimes unreliable manner, which didn't necessarily correspond to the facts on the ground. Some blocks didn't even register on this map simply because Eric never paid attention to them, while others enjoyed merely a hazy existence, waxing or waning in intensity based on their degree of interest to Eric at any given moment. What really mattered were what Eric called "the permanent establishments," their hours of opening and accessibility, and what was going on in them. Eric knew all relevant information about The Book Bunker, the secondhand emporium where he had bought and sold many items; Vic's Vinyl, where he had done the same thing; the diners, cafes and ethnic eateries he frequented; the video store where he rented classic, respectable, and not so respectable movies; the supermarket, the clothing and hardware stores, and also such locations as provided for an appealing aesthetic stroll – the harbor from which he watched the yachts out on the lake, looking like seagulls slowly moving against a rippling blue sky; ivy-covered rowhouses on quiet side streets; the Arabesque façade and atmospheric nocturnal lighting of the local 1920s movie palace, now a shopping center.

Wilson Beefheart was the proprietor of The Book Bunker. He had been the proprietor as long as Eric could remember. A couple of Eric's teachers from high school used to go to The Book Bunker on a regular basis, long ago. They had told Eric that Beefheart had been the proprietor for as long as they could remember too. They also said that they knew some old people who had gone to The Book Bunker long ago. According to these old people, Beefheart had been the proprietor of The Book Bunker as long as anyone could remember. In short, The Book Bunker was an institution, and its status as such was embodied in its proprietor.

Nobody could remember a time when Wilson Beefheart ever looked young. He had always been a bespectacled old fellow with a tousled mop of gray hair and a Van Dyke beard. He also owned a cat, a slinky orange one. He had always owned a slinky orange cat. Rumor had it that it was the same cat over the decades, and that Beefheart had somehow figured out the secret of cat immortality.

It was Saturday, early afternoon; Eric pushed open the door to the shop, and there was Wilson Beefheart himself, sitting at a battered wooden counter piled with books of various shapes, sizes and ages. The cat was darting around on these literary piles, making practically no noise while it explored the shop in its slinky way.

"Hello, young sir," said Wilson, bellowing slightly. "How can I help you?"

"Uh, I'm looking for a rather obscure book of poetry."

Wilson scowled. He lurched forward with his hand cupped to his ear and boomed: "I cannot hear you sir!"

"I'm looking for a book of poetry," said Eric, enunciating more clearly and forcefully.

"It's called *The Darkening Ecliptic*. It was written by Ern Malley, but that's a pen name."

"*The Darkening Epileptic?*" Wilson frowned in puzzlement. "What kind of name is that for a book of poetry? It sounds medical."

"Well, it's not actually a book of poetry in the traditional sense. Also, its actual title is – "

"Then why did you call it a book of poetry?" said Wilson. The cat jumped onto the counter with a thump, as if punctuating Wilson's question.

"If you'll allow me to explain – "

"No need, I've never heard of it." Turning his head and booming into the stacks behind him: "Roscoe! Can you help this young man?"

Roscoe was one of those eternal graduate students that one sometimes finds working in used book stores. In fact, he looked a bit older than Eric, and might even have finished a doctorate; but with the academic job market the way it was now, there was scant chance of him ever finding a teaching job. At least working in a bookstore with a bunch of fellow eccentrics and unemployables was something. Eric watched as he made his way into the light, emerging from the mysterious darkness that filled the space between the shelves. He wore glasses and had a black beard – the last time Eric had seen him, it was only stubble – and smelled of pipe tobacco.

67

"You're going for the prof look now?" said Eric. "You got the jacket with the patches over the elbows yet?"

"Yeah, right," said Roscoe. "Live your dreams, eh? Now what is it you're looking for?"

Eric told him.

"Ern Malley? *The Darkening Ecliptic*? Where do you come up with this stuff?"

"It was a parody, a literary hoax. A couple of poets in Australia got together and deliberately wrote a book of bad poetry. They passed it off under the pseudonym 'Ern Malley.' It fooled a magazine editor, who published it, and all the modernist critics praised it. They thought it was a masterpiece."

"*All* the modernist critics?"

"Well, a lot of them anyway."

Roscoe was staring at him skeptically, but Eric's story was true. The incident had taken place during World War II, when two poets – James McAuley and Harold Stewart – found themselves serving together in the Australian Army. Despising what they called "the loss of meaning and craftsmanship" in poetry, they set out to play a hoax on the avant-garde literary magazine *Angry Penguins*. They invented the entire biography and oeuvre of the fictitious and recently deceased poet Ern Malley in a single day. The editor of *Angry Penguins*, Max Harris, thought he had discovered an unknown genius. He excitedly agreed to publish these deliberately obscure, cryptic, and awkward surrealist poems. To the vast embarrassment of Harris, the hoax was revealed shortly thereafter.

"*Where* did this happen?" demanded Roscoe. "In Australia? Did they even know what Modernism was? Jee *ZUS*, Kipling was Modernist. Eliot too. Eliot worked in a bank, for God's sake. It wasn't a bunch of dropouts and hippies."

"So you haven't heard of the book or the poet," retorted Eric. "What good did all that edumacation do for you?"

"Enough good to not waste my time on crap like this."

"Do you think you can order it for me?"

"If it even exists," said Roscoe. "I'll believe it when I see it."

Eric rummaged around the store for a bit. He didn't find anything he wanted, but the hunt was always a stimulating experience even if no game was caught. He decided that ordering *The Darkening Ecliptic* would constitute a worthy challenge to The Book Bunker, a way for them to prove their value as a source of obscure books. He'd return to the store later, after he got a bit more relevant information, then issue the challenge.

As Eric left the store, another customer came in. As the door slowly closed, Eric heard a bit of mumbling, followed by a booming "I cannot hear you sir!"

●

While Eric liked books enough to haunt places like The Book Bunker on a regular basis, nothing pleased him quite as much as acquiring a vinyl record in good condition, especially if there was something rare or unusual about it, and doubly especially if it was an original pressing or one known by connoisseurs to be particularly outstanding. You could read a book even if you dropped it in the bath, but a beaten-up record wasn't worth a listen. Physical condition mattered hugely with a record. Like many fanatics, Eric had worked out a system in regard to record collecting in which every detail had its place and could not be moved or removed.

A record, Eric liked to argue, was truly a *record* in more ways than one. A compact disc remained the same every single time you played it. But a vinyl record sustained imperceptibly slight damage upon each new playback. Every time you took it off the platter, it was just a tiny bit different; it was by an immeasurable degree more experienced and mature. It had been brushed by the physical world in much the same way that human beings are. It was thus a record not only of the music on it, but also of the listener's experience of the music. Eric was fonder of his worn LP of *Astral Weeks* than of any pristine CD remastering because he recognized his own history of listening in the disc's worn patches, pops and tics, and other sonic colorations. He was deeply attached to his old copy of *Rubber Soul* because, in a moment of forgetfulness, he had once put down a hot cup of coffee on the album's cover, which upon being removed left a faint halo around John Lennon's head. He remembered the moment, and he remembered the circumstances – a discussion with a friend about the best way to look like you were working, without actually doing any work. It was a discussion that he had benefited from in his "career" at Eldritch.

The Japanese have a word, *sabi*, which describes this phenomenon. *Sabi* literally means "rust," and it refers to the way that handling, the effects of time, and everyday use give an object a patina of maturity. If an art object, for instance, has been owned in succession by a number of people, it acquires *sabi* through this process of ownership. Eric had read that in a book somewhere, in the course of his Japanese studies in college. He was proud that his record collection (most of which he had bought secondhand) had *sabi*. It was also something he could boast about, thus giving his life a tiny sliver of meaning.

One of the pleasures of living where he did was that, on the weekends, Eric could make the rounds of the book and record stores, as well as whatever other odd stores, shops, emporiums, establishments, venues, and holes-in-the-wall were within walking distance in his neighborhood. Having left his favorite used book store, he had just a short walk down Clark Street to get to his favorite used record store, Vic's Vinyl.

The name wasn't entirely accurate. The shop sold CDs as well as vinyl records, along with a range of accessories, publications, and the like, all related to music. But a vinyl heart was the core and engine of the store, with Vic providing the blood and energy for that heart. Vic was a bit over fifty, bald on top, and still fit, like a track-and-field athlete who had kept himself in shape over the decades. In fact, he was not an athlete but a grad-school dropout, who had spent many years on the edge of the music and theater scene, dabbling in both without success. A natural contrarian, he had opened his record store in the early nineties, which was close to the absolute nadir of vinyl LP sales in the United States. It looked like commercial suicide at the time, yet somehow Vic had made the shop work. Record collectors from all over the Chicago area and even beyond could be found here, hoping to find that elusive piece of "wax" they'd been looking for since forever. Eric knew all this about Vic because he was one of the store's steadiest customers, and gabbing with Vic on his visits was one of the pleasures of the experience.

"Hey, Eric," said Vic from behind the counter. Eric waved hello and immediately passed by the racks of CDs at the front (the "office supplies," as he called them) as he was interested only in the LPs in the back. As usual for a weekend day, the store was populated by its characteristic eccentric clientele: aging hippies in hand-me-down clothing, young post-collegiates sporting nerd glasses and body piercings, and occasional "respectable" citizens, probably serious hobbyists, but with one or two who might have wandered in by mistake or out of curiosity. Browsing the classical section, Eric found himself staring at a Deutsche Grammophon LP of Stockhausen's *Mantra*, selling for a cool 28 bucks. The reclusive, control-freak composer had withdrawn all his old DG recordings from the market, thus driving up the prices for them. Do I really need this collector's item? Eric

71

asked himself. He decided he wasn't going to take the risk on a piece he had never actually heard, and put it back in the rack. He looked at several other records with varying degrees of interest, but put them all back and moved on to the rock-and-pop section.

Ah, The Band's self-titled album! The legendary "Brown Album" – Eric had been on the lookout for a copy for ages, and now he'd found one for only $4.99! He grabbed it greedily and made his way to the counter. Yet he couldn't help noticing that Vic's face wore a slightly concerned look.

As Eric put the record down on the counter, Vic said in a low, conspiratorial voice: "I'm gonna give you a piece of insider information. Strictly for a good customer. I wouldn't tell this to someone I didn't know. Don't buy that one."

"Why not?"

"It's not a good pressing. That's a 1974 Capitol red label. The oil crisis was happening at the time, so they were using sucky quality vinyl. That record is a victim of historical circumstances. You deserve better. If you can wait till next week, I've got a 1978 Capitol maroon label coming in, pressed at their plant in Winchester, Virginia – you can tell it's a Winchester because it's got the 'rifle' logo etched into the deadwax. It's damn near perfect. I'll set it aside just for you."

"Wow. Thanks."

"Fifteen bucks Okay for it? It's special, and I'm giving you a discount. I'd sell it for twenty or more in the shop to just anyone."

Eric's face expressed momentary hesitation. Vic put on his best stern doctor look. "This is something you have to do. Your life as a listener may depend on it."

"Alright. I'll do it."

"You know a good deal when you see one, my man! The only thing better than this would be an original Robert Ludwig green label master. But I haven't seen one of those in years, and I can tell you, it'd go for a lot more than fifteen bucks in this shop. So you're making a fine investment."

As Eric turned to go, he caught sight of Alina, the diner waitress, picking through the CDs. She saw him, smiled, and waved. An invitation, perhaps?

"Looking for anything in particular?" said Eric.

"I am seeking to improve my knowledge of classic rock," replied Alina. It sounded like a rehearsed line. She smiled slightly as she said it.

"Well, I can help you with that," said Eric. He had a good feeling about this: they'd chatted now and then at the diner, every once in a while, but only for a short time on each occasion. Now, he had a shot at something deeper. He began talking, in a general, improvisatory way, about the Beatles, the Stones and the Byrds, pointing out some essential albums ("if you're not sure you like the Stones, try the *Hot Rocks* compilation"). She knew a little of it already, mentioning that she used to love the Beatles back when she was still living in Russia. Eventually, they wound up in a little café around the corner, conversing over a simple lunch.

●

When Alina Khlebnikova heard Eric complain about "The Great Displacement," she savored the irony. When Eric used the term, he was referring to an extension of his commute to work. Alina knew that her displacement was much greater than Eric's. When she was young and living in Moscow, her native country – which bore the oddly bureaucratic name of the Workers' Council [*Soviet*] Union – was dissolved by its own leadership, and its constituent republics became independent states. A few years after that, Alina made her own Great Displacement, across the ocean to another continent.

She had learned the great lesson that stability cannot be taken for granted. In fact, she doubted that stability even made sense as a concept; it seemed to her that it was merely a façade that hid the complex processes that ate away at the reality beneath, perpetually weakening it until the façade fell off. The Workers' Council Union felt stable until it wasn't. It was hardly unique: any number of states had been stable until they weren't – the empires of the Romans, Aztecs and Austro-Hungarians; the republics of Venice and the Netherlands; and so on and so forth. History and her own experience taught her that stability was an illusion.

The United States was a country she did not see until she moved there, but when she was growing up, a consistent picture of it was painted for her in school and in the media. It was like an enormous feudal property where a decadent upper class lived off the labor of the masses. A large population of minorities was permanently oppressed, and most people of all racial, ethnic and sexual backgrounds lived in constant fear of the future. A few progressives tried to organize the masses for the overthrow of capitalism, but they were beaten down by constant police harassment. Religion served as a cynical means for doping the populace, making them content with their miserable lives. This picture of America was frightening, but it was also strangely familiar: described thus, it looked almost like a copy of the old, imperial Russia, as initially depicted by Bolshevik ideologues. That country was gone, replaced by a new state; would the same thing happen in America?

Later, toward the end of the 1980s, as she approached adulthood, her picture of the outside world (and the United States in particular) began to change. It was still a country with numerous flaws, but it contained admirable features as well. You didn't need a passport to travel inside the country, even if you were going from New York to Los Angeles. Ice cream came in an extraordinary variety of flavors. You

74

could buy books that trashed the country's government and its current president in any decent bookstore. At the same time, foreigners were appearing in Moscow in ever-greater numbers. Alina had met many people from socialist countries like Angola and Vietnam, but had rarely had the chance to talk to visitors from America, England and France. One thing which made her laugh was the fact that many of these Westerners had brought with them to Russia their own personal supply of toilet paper. Alina was impressed at the abundance and quality of this imperialist toilet paper, but she also came to the conclusion that these foreigners were spoiled and prissy.

From the present perspective, America looked stable, but to her annoyance, the people living there didn't think the basic principles of history applied to them. It was the 1990s, and life in the USA was good. More precisely, life was good enough for enough people that they didn't have to think of scary, complicated things like the basic principles of history.

Meanwhile, in her home country, inflation soared, crooks looted the economy, and the president – a chronic drunk who was widely regarded as a national embarrassment – bombarded his own parliament. A lot of Russians were looking to get out, primarily going to countries they had once been taught to disdain (America, Israel, Germany, Britain, Canada). Alina was one of them. It was common in the early part of the decade for men from Western countries to show up in Russia and other post-Soviet countries looking for brides. To many Western women, they were losers with low value on the marriage market; to a lot of women in Eastern Europe, they were a way to a better life.

Alina wound up married to one such specimen, a certain Steve. He brought her to live in one of the blander Chicago suburbs, a place similar to Eric's beloved Hickory Fields. She disliked having to drive everywhere, but appreciated

75

the size of the McMansion where they lived, and the general quietude and safety of the environment. Alina found Steve fairly boring, and uncultured in a way that fulfilled a certain European stereotype of Americans, but he did have a job, and initially he treated her with respect. What she didn't realize – had no way of realizing, due to the briefness of their prior acquaintance – was the extent of his boozing and drug use. It gradually got worse, and when he tried to involve her in it, she fled. Once again, stability turned out to be an illusion. For the last year and a half, she had been living in the city, sharing an apartment with a grad student and a teacher (both of them female), and trying to get her life back on track. The diner job was, she hoped, only a stepping stone: she was still in search of the right job and the right guy.

Eric wondered if he might be the right guy. She was prettier and nicer than the other waitresses at the Lakefront Diner; she had an interesting story and perspective on things. At the diner, it always seemed that Alina refilled his coffee cup more generously than the other waitresses did – a tiny detail, but one worth noting. If she were willing to overlook his general ineptitude with women, persistent selfishness, and cynical attitude, he might indeed be the right guy. And he could show her off to other people, like a rare original pressing of a classic album.

Eric wandered around the neighborhood for a bit after their lunch. He found himself in front of one of his favorite local buildings. It was an enormous apartment building on Lake Shore Drive, built probably in the 1920s, the golden age for such structures. There were grandiose buildings of this type lining the drive for miles from downtown going up the North Side, a veritable mountain range of high-rise living looming over the lakefront. This one was made of brown brick, fifteen stories high, and it stretched across an entire block. Some famous architect had designed it; Eric couldn't recall who it was.

Whenever he passed this building, Eric fantasized about living there. He imagined the view he would have from the eighth, tenth, or twelfth floor. He thought about the furnishings, the fixtures, the parties he could throw for a narrow range of guests, people who would appreciate the location and who wouldn't impose their demands on him. Maybe Alina would be there, maybe she wouldn't. He knew he would never be able to afford this place and this style of living. But he let his imagination roam, right up to the point where he realized that at the end of the road, just like at the end of all the roads he dreamed about going down, there was disappointment.

There was a strange comfort to this thought. If all roads ended in disappointment, there was no reason to have ambition and to work hard. Living for the day was enough. Eric felt justified in his choice of a detached, mellow existence. He reflected that disappointment was a much nicer thing in this day and age, and in this place, than in other times and places. It was almost like a luxury, something you could curl up with at night and cuddle, knowing that the consequences weren't really so bad.

Chapter 7.
Woody's World

As Dagwood Wellington Latour – "Woody" as he was generally known – sat in his office at the corporate headquarters of Eldritch EduWare, he had a familiar dream. In this dream, he was a student at the University of Oxford, which he had attended many years before; but today, he was sitting not in some Oxford lecture room but in a concert hall, where his body (more rotund than he recalled from his student days) was pressing against both sides of the narrow seat. On the stage was a lecturer in full academic robes, who was quizzing the audience members about something. "Mr. Blodgett," he said, "can you tell me what happens in the third book of Thucydides?"

The spectator made some apologetic hemming noises, indicating he didn't know.

"I see," said the lecturer. "I'll have to try someone else. Mr. Plunkett, can you tell me what happens in the third book of Thucydides?"

There was a pained silence, then: "I'm sorry sir, I can't."

"Haven't *any* of you done your reading for this week?" said the lecturer. He looked towards Woody's seat. "Mr. Latour," he thundered, "can *you* tell me what happens in the third book of Thucydides?"

Woody knew the answer. Eagerly he tried to blurt it out, but the lecturer vanished and was replaced by a full orchestra which began to blare out some aggressive modern composition.

Woody Latour woke up. His phone was ringing. He picked it up.

"Hey Woody, it's Mike Riordan."

"Well hello. Have you some piece of information that you wish to disgorge to me?" Woody tried to disguise the grogginess in his voice by exaggerating his usual jocular tone.

"You know we've got a meeting now?" Damn, Mike was right. Woody looked at his watch: it was just past two-thirty. His after-lunch nap had lasted over an hour! Mike continued: "We're in the conference room right now, waiting for you. Are you going to be delayed?"

"I will join you gents in a few minutes. Please prepare whatever notes are necessary, and feel free to start the discussion without me."

"We've already done that."

"Then you are making a good start. I will be with you shortly." Damn business, cutting into my peaceful afternoon, he thought. He had totally forgotten about the meeting and was slightly worried because now he couldn't remember what they were supposed to discuss. A bit of quick self-grooming was called for. He picked up his tortoiseshell mustache comb and applied it as per the designated use, then adjusted his shiny dark chocolate brown hairpiece to

ensure it was sitting snugly on top of his head. With effort
he pushed himself out of his comfy office chair. Standing, he
attempted to get some circulation going. Coffee would help,
he thought. He walked out of the office into the network
of cubicles that made up most of the second floor. Cubicle
partition walls in cool hues of blue and green greeted him.

The office next to Woody's belonged to David Chiu, Eldritch's corporate counsel. Woody poked his head in and
saw David sitting at his desk, deeply absorbed in something
on his computer. Next to him, a radio was playing a piece
of complex, polyphonic choral music. "What ho, David!"
Woody sang out.

"Hey Woody," said David, barely looking away from the
screen as Woody gravitated in his direction. "What's up?"

"Pray tell me, what is that fine music you hearken to?"

David's serious, bespectacled face gave Woody a disbelieving look. "You know, I really don't pay a lot of attention
to what's playing, specifically. I just like having it on because it helps me concentrate. As long as it doesn't have
lyrics. I find that distracting."

"It does indeed have lyrics. I am quite sure of that. It is,
after all, choral music!"

"Well yes it does, but…I think they're in Latin or something. I can't understand them, so they don't distract me."
David looked intently at his computer screen again, trying
to send Woody a message.

"I have choral music to blame for one of the worst experiences of my life," said Woody. "Did I ever tell you about it?"

David's face froze into an expressionless mask. "I don't
remember," he replied in a monotone. Instantly, he knew
that was the wrong thing to say.

"Ah well!" said Woody, rubbing his hands together with
enthusiasm. "Yes, it happened one day in 1965 – or was it
1963? At any rate, while I was in high school. I was accompanying my Aunt Gertrude to our local church one day, for

a program of what we *thought* was going to be *light* music... however, somehow we had received tickets for a different concert..."

Shortly thereafter David lost consciousness, or else blanked out for a short time. When he came to, Woody was still droning away with gusto, only now the story had changed. Now it was sometime in the 1980s, and Woody was sitting in a booth at Top Notch Beefburgers, on 95ᵗʰ Street in the Beverly neighborhood.

"... and I ordered a Ho Hum Burger, the type they were famous for. But when this burger arrived, it had Jarlsberg cheese instead of Emmental! So I asked the waitress, Who made this burger? Jose always makes my burger, isn't he working here? And she told me that Jose had died – died of a very rare tropical disease, something like beriberi or yellow fever, poor fellow! And so, after this incident, I never ordered a Ho Hum Burger again..."

He went on like this. In his left ear, David heard a smooth radio voice announcing the next piece. It was *Arcana* by Edgard Varese, an aggressive work for very full orchestra, featuring a veritable factory floor's worth of percussion. David cranked the radio volume up almost as high as it could go. As Woody continued to blather, the crushing opening theme of *Arcana* thundered out with such force that the radio vibrated like a power tool.

"Oh dear! The war has begun!" said Woody in a loud voice. "I must flee... I'll finish the story later, David! I'm sure you're just sitting on pins and needles, wondering how it turned out!" Woody looked at his watch; he was only about ten minutes late, and he could still get some coffee before heading to the conference room. David reduced the volume, pleased that it had done its work.

Freshly made, lovely, thought Woody as he stood before the coffee machine in the kitchen. He chose a ceramic cup with the words *Happiness Is Being Croatian* on it, because he couldn't bear to drink out of a Styrofoam cup. With fussy, ritualistic motions of his hands he poured the steaming black coffee into the cup, enjoying the plash and sizzle it made. After regarding with pleasure the steam that poured upwards from it, he added with care and attention a measure of sugar and more than a smidgen of half and half. With ceremonial solemnity he raised the cup and slowly flooded his oral cavity with the strong brown beverage. The sharp wake-me-up of its odor sent its distant messengers to his extremities. Woody Latour was finally ready to take on the world. Now, what was this meeting supposed to be about?

•

When Woody Latour entered the conference room, he found Eric Freeman and Mike Riordan already there. "I apologize for my tardiness. I was just finishing up a phone call to Hong Kong. Took me longer than I expected – they do know how to drive a hard bargain over there in the Orient!"

"Yes," said Mike with a smirk, "I dream about Hong Kong sometimes, too."

"Oh, you know all my tricks now! We've worked together for so long, I can't hide anything from you anymore." He settled into the chair at the head of the table and placed the *Happiness Is Being Croatian* cup in front of him. If Woody was disturbed by Mike's awareness of his habit of taking naps in his office, he didn't show it. Over the last few months, both Mike and Eric had started to suspect that not everything was quite right in Woody's relationship with reality. When Woody was hired to be the head of the Curriculum Development department, back in the Stone Age, it was understood that he was the right person for the job. After all, he had a Ph.D., as well as some high school teaching experience under his belt. Yet as time passed, less and less seemed to get done under Woody's aegis. Every few months, they had to tear up whatever material they had created, and start all over again. All kinds of objections would be raised: the lessons were too complicated for beginners; they were not culturally sensitive to a given international market; the material was good, but the cost of implementation would be too high; it looked too much like some other company's material, which would land them in legal trouble. When Woody Latour was put in charge of the project to create a new curriculum, it was called Curriculum 2000. However, as the new century approached, it became clear that the project would not be ready by 2000, so it was renamed Curriculum 21.

"Gentlemen, I would like to demonstrate something to you," said Woody. "Watch me closely. I'm sitting. Yes?"

"Well, yes," mumbled Eric.

"I can see that," said Mike.

"There is no disagreement. Good. Now watch me." He placed his chubby, squarish hands on the arms of the chair, and pushed himself up. As he rose, Eric and Mike heard a slight hiss emanating from him, as if from a mechanical device under strain. "I'm standing up," he said. He reached his full unimposing height, wavering slightly as he struggled for balance. Then he proclaimed: "I'm standing."

Eric and Mike stared at each other. Eric wondered if they were supposed to applaud. They said nothing, so Woody continued. "What I have just demonstrated to you, gentlemen, is a *system of meaning*. We use such systems in our language every day, and we don't even think about it. These systems of meaning will form the basis of our new curriculum."

"Really?" moaned Mike.

"I realize you're skeptical," said Woody, sitting down again. "I advise you to hear me out." Woody began to propound in detail on his systems of meaning. Gradually, and gaining in esoteric complication as the minutes went by, an enormous architecture of words came into being in front of Eric and Mike. In its baroque complexity, it resembled the Sanskrit grammar of Panini, Bach's *The Art of Fugue*, Raphael's *School of Athens*, and Kant's *Critique of Pure Reason*. Woody added sentence atop sentence, like a mason building up the walls of a castle. Sounds resounded against other sounds, verbs were twisted into a myriad of meanings, simple prepositions dazzled in their multifarious usages. As Woody held forth, a deep drone filled the heads of his listeners – could it be the very sound underpinning the structure of the universe?

Woody finished his disquisition, and silence reigned in the room for a minute. Eric blinked and Mike rubbed his eyes; a passerby, seeing them at that moment, would have thought both of them were awakening from a nap.

"So, what do you gents think?" asked Woody.

They tried to discuss what he had just expounded, but without much success. Eric was finding it difficult to remember what precisely Woody had just said, even though he had been impressed by its complexity, and by Woody's obvious belief in his system, when he was listening to it. Yet now that the speech was over, its details were evaporating from his memory. "That's a lot to take in, Woody," he said. "Do you have a summary of all this somewhere? Also, it might be easier to understand in graphic form."

"I may create a helpful chart for you, just to ensure we are all on the same page. Do remember, however, that Socrates himself never wrote anything down. It was all recorded by his students. Feel free to put those writing implements in your possession to good use!" Woody made some closing comments; it was clear he wanted to wrap this meeting up.

"Just one thing, Woody, before we finish," said Mike. "I have a meeting with Audrey Shroom coming up later this week. She's going to ask me how Curriculum 21 is going. What am I supposed to tell her?"

Woody looked puzzled. "I wasn't aware of a meeting with Audrey."

"Yeah, she wants to talk to me, just one to one. Maybe she assumed you were busy or something."

"Tell her that our latest strategy is promising, and we should be making progress fairly soon."

Mike and Eric sat stone-faced while Woody shuffled out of the room. This was more pressure from the top. Rumors had drifted down to their department to the effect that the upper management at Furuhashi were having their doubts about the long-term viability of the company. Eldritch had been acquired almost as an afterthought, a cheaply gained prize during Furuhashi's inroads into the North American market, where their interests were more concentrated in media and related service industries. The management in Tokyo knew that Eldritch had some value in servicing the constantly growing market of foreign language learners in East Asia, where the appetite for English in particular seemed to be limitless. Yet to date, their investment in the company was showing no signs of paying off.

They had reacted by doing some reshuffling at the top. Audrey Shroom, in her late thirties and boasting an MBA, had been brought in as managing director. There was some resentment in the company at seeing this relatively young outsider being given the top job. The air of mystery that surrounded her didn't help her gain the trust of the veteran employees. She spent most of her time in her office with the door closed, meeting with people on a one-to-one basis. Few announcements of any specificity were forthcoming from that office, leading to speculation as to what was going on in there. As often happens when people want to speculate, but have little concrete information to speculate about, their thoughts dwelled on trivia. In Audrey's case, speculation focused on her unusual last name. Some people thought it was Slavic in origin (*Szrum* or *Šrum*, possibly even *Шрум*). Others insisted it had to be German (*Schrum*). Still others believed that it had no particular ethnic origin, but had been made up by some joker of an official at Ellis Island who couldn't pronounce an unusual name. To make matters worse, a rumor was circulating that Audrey had begun her career in the mailroom before working her way up. As a result, some people had dubbed her "Audrey Shroom from the mailroom." Other employees started repeating it just because they liked the way it sounded. She had heard them do it once or twice, and it irritated her. In fact, there was no evidence that she had ever worked in a mailroom. Anyone meeting Audrey for the first time was warned not to mention the mailroom in her presence.

"What are you going to tell her?" asked Eric.

"What can I say?" said Mike. "Sooner or later, Woody will have to be implicated in this. I can't cover for him forever. After a while, it starts to make the whole department look bad. And that means us."

"At the same time, criticizing Woody runs the risk of making *us* look bad. They could rationally say, let's hold on to Woody – he's got the credentials, the track record, what have you – and get rid of his non-performing underlings."

Mike permitted a wry smile to cross his face. "There's no way out. We're doomed."

Eric decided to pour himself some more coffee and get back to work. By the time he returned to his desk, an idea had seized him. "That's it," he said to himself. "It's time for me to protest. But I'm going to do it in an erudite manner, befitting the goals this company has set for itself." After a brief check on the Internet – he wanted to be sure of the correct spelling of the phrase – he sat down in front of his computer, opened a new Word document, and in 72-point type, wrote the following sentence:

LASCIATE OGNI SPERANZA, VOI CH'ENTRATE!

He printed it out, and stuck it high on the partition next to his cubicle. It was a safe, timid kind of protest. It was rare for a management person from outside the department to venture as far as Eric's cubicle, and any who did would be unlikely to know what the phrase meant anyway.

Mike walked over and took a look. "What's this?"

"It's from *The Divine Comedy*," said Eric. "The *Inferno*. It says: 'Abandon all hope, you who enter here.' It's written over the gates of Hell."

"Medieval Italian. Great. When Woody sees it, he will finally be able to put that Ph.D. in Romance languages to practical use. Whether it will cause him to reflect on where we're going with this stupid curricular project – that's a different story."

Chapter 8.

Not Sex

On the night before Eric was scheduled to give a presentation to his department (to be joined by a special guest), he had a disturbing dream. In this dream, he had been contracted by a local college to teach an obscure African language. The fact that he had no knowledge of the language was not considered to be an obstacle because, as the dean explained to him, "The students won't know the difference."

But when class began there were unforeseen complications. Eric found that pretending to know the language was no substitute for actually knowing it. In class, he kept sneaking looks at the dictionary and grammar while trying not to appear totally clueless. The students seemed aware of his lack of knowledge, and tormented him with pointless questions like, "How do you say 'I had oatmeal for breakfast today'?" He gave up trying to answer these questions and decided to have everyone count to five. However, he could remember only the words for two (*huaro*) and three (*poitoin*). He repeated these numbers until the dream ended.

"Thank God it was only a dream," he mumbled when he got up. Since he had dawdled in bed a few minutes longer than usual, he had to rush to make the train. He grabbed the videocassette he needed for the presentation from its resting place next to the VCR, shoved it into his bag, and left.

•

The attendees were already in the conference room: Mike Riordan, Woody Latour, and the rep from eSchooling Online. Woody was telling some interminable story about his days at Oxford to Mr. Quarles, the eSchooling rep. Having found out that Mr. Quarles was a mere graduate of a directional state university, Woody was establishing his own superiority through this meandering series of anecdotes, which somehow managed to bundle together various features of Oxford life, including punting on the Thames, the difficulties of using the Bodleian Library, and the cantankerous persona of Sir Hugh Lloyd-Jones, the Regius Professor of Greek at Christ Church. Mr. Quarles nodded and smiled in what he thought were the right places, but you could tell he was faking it. When Eric burst in, videotape and notebook in hand, Mr. Quarles looked relieved.

"Okay," Eric began, switching on the big TV/VCR combo, "I'm glad to see you all here. This video that I'm going to show you is in two parts. The first part demonstrates some of the old-fashioned methods of pedagogy that a lot of schools still employ. The second part shows how these methods can be streamlined and improved." He shoved the video into the slot and pressed "play." Thumping electronic music blared from the television.

"That's a bit aggressive for an educational video," said Mike. Eric wasn't paying attention; he was going over his notes in preparation for the first scene. The screen showed a couple of women in bikinis relaxing by the side of a pool. A grungy-looking guy with long hair and tattoos on his pumped-up arms, clad only in cutoff jeans, wandered into the scene. Unusual names flashed across the screen – Tiffany Phoenix, Vikki Lynxx, Diego St. Clair – as the music subsided.

"I say, that doesn't look very much like old-fashioned pedagogy," commented Woody. "I'm quite an old-fashioned fellow myself, and I can tell you that I wasn't allowed near the pool until I'd learned my French irregular verbs."

"Huh?" Eric looked up from his notes. "Oh, shit," came out of him involuntarily as he was overcome by a wave of nausea. Instead of the demonstration video, he had brought with him the previous night's porno movie.

"Hey, what are you ladies up to?" asked the grungy man on the screen, in a flat voice. The trio around the table watched the proceedings with the bemused, placid look that Eric called "conference face." Apparently the truth of the situation had not yet hit them.

"Oh, it's so hot out here," moaned one of the girls. "Maybe I should take off – "

With trembling fingers Eric pressed the stop button. "As you can see, a lot of people nowadays think learning should be fun," he blurted. "Yes, hanging out at poolside – that's supposed to help us learn!" He pressed the fast-forward button, since he couldn't think of anything else to do. It occurred to him to plead technical difficulty. "Sorry, this tape has been acting up. Now if you'll bear with me a minute…" He positioned himself in front of the screen, so that only he could see it. "This video doesn't exactly match the notes I made, so I'll have to find…" His voice was cracking; he needed water.

"I say, what was that tattooed fellow doing?" asked Woody. "It looked like he was up to no good."

"He *was*," said Eric, "he hadn't done his homework!" Eric started playing with the buttons on the VCR, pushing and poking them busily, to give the impression that he was trying to fix things. After a bit of this strategic poking, he gave up. "Hm, this doesn't seem to be working too well," he said as he ejected the tape from the machine.

"Hey Eric, you want me to help out?" asked Mike.

"No, no, that's not necessary," said Eric. "I think I've got it all figured out." With his back turned to his audience, he examined the underside of the cassette, and using his pen he tore at the tape inside, mangling it in a few strokes. "Aw, will you look at this!" He held up the cassette for all to see. "It's twisted. It won't play properly."

The audience's conference face gave way to a look of disappointment. Everybody nowadays seemed to love visual presentations. Now, they would have to watch a guy speaking from notes.

"I'm sorry about this," said Eric. His voice was still dry, but he recovered his composure and managed to finish the presentation. Afterwards, he worried about the impression his nervousness had made, and whether anyone had seen him deliberately mangling the tape. He realized to his annoyance that the video store would charge him for the cost of the mangled tape, but given the circumstances, he doubted he could have acted differently.

•

The Angry Ghost was just off Belmont, in an area known for its used clothing stores, coffee houses, and oddball shops selling everything from vintage sports memorabilia to sex toys. Every now and then on the weekends, it was known to host an open mic poetry and music show, under the aegis of none other than David Chiu, the corporate counsel at Eldritch EduWare. Since everyone needs a hobby, he had started up the open mic nights at The Angry Ghost. Eric had been to these events once or twice, and vaguely remembered that they were a source of good, relaxed fun, if not much else. Since the acts didn't demand the total attention of the audience (you could still chat while the performance was going on), it seemed like a good venue for a first date.

"How's it going?" said Eric, as he and Alina looked around for a table in the rapidly populating club.

"Good, except for one thing," said David. "Is there any way you can get Woody Latour to move to another office, so he's not next door to me? I've had to listen to more stories in the last few months than in my entire life before we moved to the new place."

Eric laughed loudly and shamelessly. "Man, I think more people should experience Woody's storytelling talents. The whole company can benefit from them. Just think of it as an ongoing seminar on corporate communications."

"Well, that's easy for you to say. I'm going to invest in some industrial-strength earplugs." They dropped that unpleasant subject; Eric introduced Alina, and David gave her some basic information on the acts that would be performing tonight. They sat down and waited for the show to begin.

The lights dimmed. First up was Philaster the Incredible. He was a young man with an explosive mop of curly black hair, the springiness of which was enhanced by the multicolored propeller beanie perched atop his head. He had an angry look on his face and wore a black T-shirt that featured a picture of a fist and the words *Make Change Happen Now*, all in a livid shade of yellow. Philaster started out with a passionate poetic denunciation of consumerism, then slid into a lengthy autobiographical monologue that somehow managed to indict his abusive parents, his abusive friends, the abuse he had suffered at school, and the multiple abuses he had to endure at his current job. He punctuated this symphony of suffering with random shouts and gestures, creating a strong impression of someone having a fit. The audience of fifty or so people nodded in the right places and tried to look sympathetic, but they did it in a perfunctory manner, like employees at a meeting listening to the boss give a speech, putting on their best business face to avoid looking disloyal. At least, that's the metaphor that went through Eric's mind.

"Does he think he's actually going to make change happen now with monologues like that?" Eric said to Alina. She chuckled. Philaster ended his performance, and the audience signaled its relief with tepid applause. David Chiu got up to introduce the next act. This was Rosie, Princess of the Amazon. In reality, Rosie looked like a white girl from the suburbs, maybe fourteen years old at most; she had piled her dark hair into a column and put on a pristine white gown, which made her look disturbingly like a child bride. As she began to talk about herself in a squeaky voice, Eric was startled to hear her say that she had begun performing "when I was in college" – either she was some kind of prodigy, or she was much older than she looked.

Judging by the quality of her performance, it was the latter. Rosie's specialty was "rapping about relationships." This mainly consisted of spastic verses, delivered in a stuttering tone with no concern for rhyme, rhythm or even basic articulation, denouncing various men who had done her wrong. It was unnerving to think of this childlike individual involved in such an unhealthy manner with adult men. On the other hand, she might have been making up the whole thing. This performance by Rosie, Princess of the Amazon turned out to be mercifully brief. As she slinked off the stage, she got even less applause than Philaster the Incredible had.

93

The two opening acts were followed by a couple of others, equally dismal. One involved a middle-aged man with a beard reciting poetry while strumming a guitar, looking very retro like a 1960s folk singer; the other was some kind of individual spewing out "transgressive" verses while dressed in a clown suit. Eric and Alina missed whatever benefits might have been engendered by a deeper engagement with these performers because they were making small talk, having lost interest in the show. Alina was talking about her job in the diner, but Eric was only directing about one-third of his attention capacity to her. Another third went toward keeping a lazy watch on the antics occurring on stage, and the third third was taken up with his feelings of regret at having invited Alina to this open mic poetry night in the first place. He contemplated the menu, pretending to be interested, while thinking it was time to ditch The Angry Ghost and go somewhere else.

The small talk and division of attention meant that Eric and Alina missed the introduction of the next act. When they next looked at the stage, they saw two rather androgynous-looking adults standing on it, both of them of medium height or less, their hair cut short and stiff, and both dressed in matching steel-gray pantsuits. They looked like a pair of unionized workers out of some midcentury industrial film.

"I am Dean," announced the one on the left, in a metallic tenor voice.

"I am Deanna," announced his partner, in a metallic soprano voice.

"And we are Canned Meat," they chimed together. Eric's music-nerd gene suggested the name was some sort of tribute to the blues-rock band Canned Heat, but he was immediately disabused of this idea. "We are Canned Meat," said Dean, "because like you, like all humanoids, we are pieces of meat, pushed and forced into places and positions we never chose and never wanted to be in. We are bottled, we are caged, we are chopped down to size and put in a box, we are canned, sold, and thrown away. We dedicate this performance to all of our canned brothers and sisters."

"God *damn*, this is pretentious," muttered Eric. "Get a job, will ya." A couple of people at a nearby table overheard him and smiled. Dean said, "We will now perform for you the most famous sentence spoken so far this year. It was pronounced by the President of the United States on January 26. That sentence is 'I did not have sexual relations with that woman'."

A slight sense of unease on the part of the audience was palpable. Were they about to be subjected to a Republican propaganda attack? But then Canned Meat launched into their performance. "I did not have sexual," said Dean in his robotic voice, and Deanna immediately completed the sentence: "relations with that woman." With great speed and agility, they broke down the sentence into its component parts, hurling the words at each other, pretending to catch them and then hurling them back, sometimes reciting a word or two simultaneously before diverging again. Every now and then a word was stressed or emphasized, by shouting, or by bellowing it out an octave lower or higher than usual. After a minute or two of this, the effect it created was of a bell-like but irregular ringing.

with that woman with that woman with THAT woman with THAT woman with that woman

Alina exclaimed: "They are rapping, I think!" She was happy to show off her knowledge of American pop culture idiom. But Eric the music nerd knew they weren't rapping; they were "phasing." This technique was associated with Steve Reich's pieces of the 1960s, where two instruments would repeat identical patterns over and over again, while subtle tempo shifts brought them out of sync with each other, and then into sync again. There was also an echo of the *Klangfarbenmelodie* of the Second Vienna School, whereby a melody would be broken up among multiple instrumental lines. But this was the first time Eric had heard two voices doing this, rather than instruments.

relations relations relations reLAtions reLAtions relations relations reLAtions reLAtions

The audience was actually paying attention this time; all eyes were fixed on the stage, all ears were taking it in. Canned Meat continued to build sound patterns out of Bill Clinton's simple denial of marital infidelity with breathtaking speed and virtuosity. Eventually they settled on two syllables: *not* and *sex*. "I did *not not not not not not not not not not not not not* ..." spat out Dean at high speed, while Deanna, in a machine-gun staccato, ground out "... have *sex sex sex sex sex sex sex sex sex sex sex*...." They must have repeated these syllables hundreds of times in a row, while phasing in and out of each other's rhythm. The ringing sound continued, but it had changed into something else; now it was less like a bell and more like a pulsating and echoing electronic signal. The phasing climaxed with a rapid-fire enunciation of these two syllables: *not sex not sex not sex not sex not sex not sex notsex notsex notsexnotsexnotsexnotsex* ... And with a jointly shouted *sex!* the performance ended.

The room erupted noisily in possibly the first instance of sincere applause since the evening began. Canned Meat took a bow and moved off the stage. David Chiu announced that there would be a short break before the remaining acts came on. Canned Meat came out from the wings to mingle with the crowd for a short while. Eric and Alina approached them.

"You guys were terrific," said Eric.

"Yes, really," added Alina. "I never saw something like that before. How did you start? Are you brother and sister?"

"We're not brother and sister," said Dean, "even though we may look like it." It was slightly disconcerting to hear that his normal, off-stage speaking voice had that metallic ring. Maybe it was his natural tone of voice, and he had decided to make the most of it. Or perhaps he had been phasing so long that it had permanently altered his voice.

"We've been playing a number of venues," said Deanna, who had the same metallic speaking voice. "Just for the exposure. And the experience. Some of them are more serious than this one."

Eric asked about their history and upcoming projects.

"At first we called ourselves Nicotine," said Deanna. "Because we were selling ourselves as an addictive substance. But then we realized that people might think we were promoting smoking, and we didn't want them to get that idea. So we changed our name to Canned Meat. It's like we were making a statement about the human condition."

"We phase about all kinds of things," said Dean. "The environment, relations between the sexes, consumerism ... a broad spectrum. One of our upcoming projects is to phase some key phrases from the Universal Declaration of Human Rights."

•

Eric and Alina wound up at a café that stayed open late. It was that time of night when your vision begins to take on a hazy glow, even if you're not seriously drunk or suffering from a mental condition. A couple of tables away, a man with unruly gray hair was eating bacon and eggs. The man was dressed in a brown bathrobe over purple pajamas, and his feet were shod in big hiking boots. Just before he dug into the eggs, he sprinkled them with tabasco sauce.

"I have learned to embrace the craziness," said Alina. She made it sound like a credo. "It is interesting at least. I have a literary project right now. I write a series of sketches about some of the people I meet when I'm working at the diner. Especially on the late shift. The crazy people, the – what's this word, essentrics?"

"Eccentrics."

"Yes, the eccentrics. The people with strange habits and obsessions. You forget the normal customers. But you don't forget the eccentrics. Those are the people I write about. If you want people to remember you, be eccentric."

"Oh, I see now," said Eric. "I'm one of those eccentrics, with my crazy vinyl collecting and my weird social events. That's why we're talking. I'm your subject matter!"

"Please, you are not weird enough for my sketchbook. Not yet. Maybe you will be if you work on it."

"You know, some record collectors are so obsessed with records as art objects, they buy certain records only for the jackets. That is, they throw away the record and then hang the jacket on their wall like a work of art."

"Do you do that?"

"Not yet."

"Then you are really not weird enough for me. If you start doing this, and make your apartment into a gallery of record jackets, then you will be weird enough and I will write about you."

"Maybe you should sit down with Canned Meat for an interview and write about them," suggested Eric.

"Canned Meat reminds me of *zaum* poetry," said Alina.

"They remind you of zoom poetry? What's zoom poetry?"

"*Za OOM*," she said, enunciating carefully. "Now I wish I didn't say that. Because now I have to explain it, and I think you won't understand even the explanation. In Russia, there was the Silver Age, in literature. They wrote *zaum* poetry. This word *zaum* means 'beyond the mind' or 'beyond reason.' They used sounds that were familiar from normal language, but in completely new ways."

"New ways?" said Eric. "Can you give an example?"

Alina looked at him dubiously. "Well… yes, but I don't think you will understand." She screwed her face into a look of fierce concentration and emitted a series of syllables. To Eric, they sounded vaguely Slavic, while also evoking something like a primitive incantation delivered by a person suffering from a speech impediment.

"Hm," mused Eric. "I see what you mean. I think."

"Your problem is that you don't know Russian, so you have no context. The author of that poem is Aleksei Kruchonykh. He said there is more of *real* Russian language in it than in all the works of Pushkin."

"Well, I guess he would know. But thanks for making me feel inadequate."

"You *did* ask for an example; I gave it to you. But I knew you won't understand it," she said, smiling beatifically. "But you see, it *goes beyond*. It's beyond normal language. It gives you feelings and ideas you don't normally get from just words. That's what Canned Meat were doing. Well, not exactly, but it was something similar."

"Forget about them and about zoom poetry, too. That's too complicated for your sketchbook. Maybe you should talk to the guy in the pajamas, right over there. You know who you would like? Evan Jarrett. I think you saw him already – I bought him breakfast at the Lakefront, and you served us. The 'Philosopher and Activist' as he calls himself."

"Oh yes. I think I remember him. I'm writing in English, it's good practice and it forces me to think harder about what I want to say. Writing in not your native language is helpful that way."

The conversation continued, but fatigue gradually overtook them, and they left. Eric said goodbye. He said he'd call her again, but in his own mind, he wasn't quite certain about that. Relationships required an awful lot of work, and his capacity for work was very limited.

Chapter 9.

S h a f u

When Eric Freeman entered the Eldritch building, he found David Chiu in the lobby, waiting for the elevator. Eric didn't really want to talk to David (or anyone) right now – he was not a very sociable person in the morning – but he couldn't hide. He knew what David was going to say, and that he would have to make small talk about it.

"Hey there, Eric," said David as they got in the elevator. "How'd you like Open Mic Night at The Angry Ghost?"

"It was fun," Eric replied diplomatically. "But that couple, Canned Meat – they were really impressive." At least this observation was sincere. Ever since their performance, bits of their act had been running through his head in an on-again, off-again loop. "Truly a unique ensemble."

"They are indeed," said David. "Really talented and unique, as you say. I expect them to go far."

*not sex not sex not sex not sex not sex notsex notsex not-
sexnotsexnotsex*

The door opened on the second floor. "See you later," said
Eric, as he stepped out.

"Same to you," said David, heading to his office.

with that woman with that woman with that woman

Mike was already at his station, as was usually the case;
it was a rare thing for Eric to come in earlier than Mike. Eric
went through the Routine, then found himself wondering
what to do next. Today was one of those days when there
wasn't an obvious piece of work demanding immediate
attention. One way of dealing with such days was to dip
into one's backlog of work, the kind connected to long-term
projects and ideas that needed development, and see what
you could get done. Another way was to goof off. Since Mike
appeared to be surfing the Internet rather than working,
Eric went for the second option. He stood up and walked
over to Mike's cubicle.

"Hey Mike, is Woody in today?" he asked.

"Absent without leave once again. Probably having a
very long, very luxurious breakfast somewhere."

"You up for a round?"

Mike turned decisively away from the computer. "You
bet."

Although Mike was a quiet guy, a family man and dedicated to his job, Eric had been able to connect to him on one
thing: cinephilia. They were both movie lovers, favoring the
classic and the foreign over current Hollywood products.
While Eric appreciated movies as an escape from his present life (which was how he regarded practically all aesthetic
experiences), for Mike it was a little more wistful, as he had
once harbored ambitions in this area, even shooting a few
short films in his younger days. But those dreams died, and
now he was occupying a cubicle at an increasingly stagnant
enterprise, housed in a large metal box in one of the boxier

Chicago suburbs. Work, and the demands of home and family, soaked up all his energy. As he once said to Eric in a moment of exasperation: "At work I look forward to dinner, at dinner I look forward to watching TV, when I'm watching TV, I look forward to sleep...it's only when sleeping that I don't look forward to anything." In such a situation, the occasional do-nothing day at the office was a gift.

To break up the corporate monotony, Eric had devised a game called "First Shot – Last Shot." Beginning as a simple quiz, a test of the other's knowledge, it had ramified and evolved over the last few months, constantly gaining in rules and complexity. Since there was no urgent work this morning, and they were both enjoying an extended coffee break, Eric thought it would be a good time for another round of the game.

"Okay," he said, "let's roll. An X-ray of a cancer patient's stomach." He sipped his coffee while waiting for Mike's reply.

Mike looked flummoxed for a second, then recovered. "I might know this, but I need a clue. I'm willing to lose a point for it."

"Okay. The clue is 'Japan'."

"Got it," said Mike. "It's Kurosawa. *Ikiru*."

"Brilliant!" said Eric. "Now tell me: is it the first shot or the last shot?"

"Damn, it's been so long...I'm gonna say last shot."

Eric put on his best disappointed teacher face. "Really? How can you say that? The guy is dead at the end of the film. You didn't think the X-ray was some kind of flashback, did you? Only one point out of two for you. Now take your own shot!"

Mike thought for a second, then said: "A helicopter transporting a statue of Jesus out of a city."

"Oh come on, that's one of the most famous shots ever. *La Dolce Vita*, first shot. Three points for me!"

"No, two points for you. I thought we agreed that not needing a clue didn't entitle you to an extra point."

"Did we agree on that? I don't remember. Come to think of it, I don't know if we actually wrote the rules down. Maybe we should. Anyway, I'll give you the benefit of the doubt. Two points for me."

"Okay," said Mike. "Your shot again."

"A man on a horse, with a donkey following right behind, going through a heavily forested landscape. The wind is howling, and a Leonard Cohen song is playing on the soundtrack."

"Oh hey, I just watched this!" exclaimed Mike. "*McCabe & Mrs. Miller*. And it's the first shot."

"Two points for you," said Eric.

The game went on for a while, until they both got tired of it. In the running total they had been keeping, Eric was slightly ahead. This was no surprise, as he had more free time to indulge his interests.

After they finished "First Shot – Last Shot," Eric remembered that he had a few pieces of backlog work to attend to. The first thing he wanted to do was get in touch with Paul Frumkin, the philosophy professor who had responded to Eldritch's ad for freelancers. Eric had dawdled over this assignment for some time, but now he had a better idea of what sort of work he wanted from the freelancers, and he intended to do a little brainstorming with the professor over the phone. He located Frumkin's application in the huge pile that occupied a corner of his desk, found his phone number, and dialed.

Three sharp, rising tones, followed by an unpleasant female voice: "The number you have reached has been disconnected." She did not say what the new number was. Eric next tried the switchboard number for Eastbrook College. He was referred to the faculty number for the humanities departments. He got another female voice, but this time it belonged to an actual human being.

"I'd like to speak to Dr. Paul Frumkin, please."

"I'm sorry," said the woman, "Dr. Frumkin no longer works here."

"What, in the department?"

"No, in the college. He is no longer employed by Eastbrook College."

"Really? Can you tell me what happened to him?"

"Who am I speaking to, please?"

Eric told her who he was and why he was calling.

"I'm afraid I can't give out any more information about this, due to our confidentiality policy. And if his home phone was disconnected, I guess he's moved. I wish I could be more helpful."

"Thanks anyway." He threw Frumkin's application back on the pile, and wondered who he should try next. Maybe Sanjay?

•

After lunch the same day, as Eric was walking past the long bulletin board just outside the cafeteria, his attention was snagged by a number of fresh postings. The first was the slogan in big blocky letters across the top: *It is ATTITUDE and not APTITUDE that determines ALTITUDE.* A couple of the departments had recently held a seminar led by a consulting firm, a manifestation of that mystifying phenomenon whereby companies are persuaded to part with considerable sums of money, in exchange for programs consisting half of platitudes and half of game-playing. The slogan was one of the beliefs that the seminar was trying to inculcate, and somebody in the management obviously thought that it was a piece of wisdom worthy of being propagated throughout the company. If a company had money to burn, perhaps it could find an excuse for the expense of hiring these consulting firms; but for a business like Eldritch, this was one discretionary budget item that hardly justified itself.

Below the slogan, several pieces of paper were posted on the board. All of them were white with black type, arranged in such a way that it looked like poetry. As Eric looked closer, he realized that they were the entries in the company song contest.

Herb Pforzheim, an accountant on the third floor whom Eric barely knew, had submitted a song with the indication "to be sung to the tune of 'I've Been Workin' on the Railroad'." Herb's new lyrics went like this:

I've been workin' here at Eldritch,
From Monday to Friday;
I've been workin' here at Eldritch,
Just to pass the time away.

Eric felt acute embarrassment for Herb and wanted to burst out laughing at the same time. A shudder of shock went through him at the notion that a respectable bald middle-aged man, with a family and a career to protect, could have posted such drivel for everyone to see. The first line, granted, was unimaginative, but at least it was not terrible. The second line, however, scanned so badly that no vocalist in the world could have made it sound right. The third simply repeated the first, and the fourth was ridiculous: no one worked at Eldritch "just to pass the time away," with the possible exception of Woody Latour. Eric thought of replacing the line with "just to earn a good day's pay," but he recoiled at the idea of getting into the spirit of things.

The Japanification of Eldritch is proceeding apace, thought Eric with a sigh, and it probably wasn't even the fault of the absentee management back in Tokyo. Most likely, the guilty party was some eager beaver who had read one book about Japanese management techniques, and

decided that team-building measures like a company song
contest would help Eldritch to blast its way boldly into the
future – as a certain currently embattled President put it,
"to build a bridge to the twenty-first century." This beaver
presumably had the ear of Audrey Shroom; Eric doubted
that Audrey was imaginative enough to come up with such
a thing on her own, although he had to admit that he didn't
know her very well. The purpose of the song was to promote
shafu ("company spirit"). At a certain point, all workers,
high or low, senior or junior, boardroom or mailroom, would
be required to memorize this song, and even sing it at appropriate moments. *And I'm already commuting over an
hour to get out here, just like they do in Tokyo. Plus, I've
got that damn calendar!*

To Eric's amazement, Herb's song got even worse:

Can't you hear the salesmen calling,
"Send us out to sell some more"?
Can't you hear the accountants saying,
"We're the ones who keep the score"?

Enough! thought Eric. He walked away shaking his
head. The ongoing decay and dysfunction at Eldritch, he
decided, were rooted in superficiality, but it was a superficiality that went two ways. On the one hand, there were
eager local managers trying to force-feed Japanese concepts of efficiency and *shafu* to American employees who
– through no fault of their own – were unable to implement
them in a coherent way. On the other hand, the Japanese
management, faced with a situation they didn't really understand, fell back on simplifications. That must have been
how Woody Latour got hired in the first place: because he
fit somebody's preconceived notions of what an eccentric,
innovative Western genius had to be like. Woody's affec-
tations, mused Eric, must have struck the managers as

genuine erudition. Meanwhile, the gradual ungluing of Woody from reality was starting to have consequences, and the managers, whether in Boxville or Tokyo, still had no clear idea what to do about it.

•

Another Saturday evening, and Evan, being impecunious and having almost no social life, found himself without plans of any kind. He had spent the afternoon walking along the lakefront with no clear goal in mind, other than to gain some inspiration from his surroundings. The area he explored was once a prestigious resort spot, anchored by the sunrise-yellow Edgewater Beach Hotel; movie stars, presidents, big bands, and other celebrities had once passed through this place, one of the most impressive creations of the architect Benjamin Marshall. The hotel had suffered the fate of so many distinguished buildings: it had been demolished and replaced by high-rise condominiums, but the palatial Edgewater Beach Apartments (in sunset pink, meant to provide a counterpoint to the color of the hotel) still stood there; the sight of this massive structure, along with the sonic accompaniment of the crashing waves on the beach, which gave a sense of nature in motion, made him feel a little more connected to the world, more of a participant in life. Sunrise was long gone, only sunset remained; he wondered if this meant that the last day in the history of the world was ending. Walking around eventually bored him and drained off his excess energy, and when the sun went down and the world didn't come to an end, he decided to go home.

As he opened the front door, he found Isaiah, the Nigerian former law student, checking his mailbox. He was carrying a couple of plastic bags labelled "Dragon's Garden," the name of the Chinese restaurant where he worked. "Hi,

Isaiah," said Evan. "What, are you delivering food to your own home?"

"Freebies, man," said Isaiah. "It's one of the few benefits I get out of this place. You want some kung pao?"

"That'd be great, thanks a lot." Isaiah handed over one of the bags. "How much longer are you working at that joint?" asked Evan. "I thought you'd be out of there by now."

"Longer than I ever expected," replied Isaiah with a trace of exasperation. "The plan is to do law school again – I need an American degree – but money's tight."

"Good luck to you. I really appreciate the free food."

"And how are things with you?"

For about three seconds, Evan considered how he should respond to this question. The truth was that things with him were difficult and complex. A recent incident flashed through his mind. As a philosopher and activist, Evan was aware that he had to get his name and face out there in the world in order to have some practical effect. For this purpose, he approached a large, well-funded suburban library with a proposal: Would they be open to hosting a series of lectures based on the chapters of his current philosophical treatise in progress? Since his eventual goal was to publish *The Positive Life*, this would be an ideal way to air his ideas before a live audience composed of interested people. The librarian that he approached took a close look at him, then asked some basic questions about his educational background and publication record. At that point Evan's initiative faltered and he excused himself, saying he would send her all the information she wanted in a more detailed, user-friendly form.

The librarian sent him away gently, as if she didn't want to embarrass him ("I look forward to getting that information packet from you"). As he walked out of the library in defeat, he felt like kicking himself for his lack of preparedness. If he wanted to succeed at projects like this, either he had to come up with a really convincing way of selling the truth about himself, or he had to become a creative and shameless liar. Sadly, his skills in both departments needed a lot of work.

"Things are alright," was what Evan finally told Isaiah. "Could be worse. I'm keeping busy." Trying to explain his situation to people he barely knew seemed like an utter waste of time. He said goodbye to Isaiah and went on his way.

As Evan walked down the hall to his apartment, he saw a woman perched on her knees in front of Jeff and Nancy's door. The woman was fortyish, fairly short, and her tousled brown hair was falling in front of her face. She was staring hard at the door. As Evan walked by, she flipped the hair out of her face, turned to Evan and said in a worried voice, "Call 911."

"What?" said Evan. "Why?"

"I'll explain," said the woman. "Just call, and I'll do the talking."

Damn, modern life can be stressful, thought Evan as he opened the door. He put down the bag of Chinese food and then went directly to the phone. The woman didn't look dangerous, he thought; it should be safe to let her into the apartment. Anyway, if she wanted to steal something, why would she call 911?

The operator came on. "I've got a situation here," said Evan, and gave the address. The woman had already zipped into the apartment and was right by the phone. Evan gave it to her.

"It's my ex-husband," she said. "He won't let me see my kid. He's got him locked up in his apartment and won't let him out."

Evan edged away, back out into the hall. He sensed that the latest episode of *The Jeff & Nancy Show* was about to begin, this evening with two special guests. Already, nervous talking noises were emanating from behind the door, still fairly muffled, but now some young-boy interjections were added. "I don't *wanna!*" shot out suddenly in a prepubescent alto.

"Just shut up, Jimmy!" said Nancy sharply.

Evan came back into the apartment. The woman was still talking, in a speedy, breathless voice. "Jeff, Jeff Morton, that's his name... no, but he gets aggressive when he drinks... yes, they live together, right here, and Jimmy is stuck there and he can't get out... no, I'm calling from the apartment next door..."

Evan, listening to her ramble, put together the pieces of the "situation." Valerie (the woman's name) had divorced Jeff and got some kind of split-custody deal regarding their small son, Jimmy. Today, Jimmy was supposed to be with Valerie, but jealous Jeff had abducted Jimmy and barricaded the both of them in his apartment, together with Nancy. It was two against one, and the poor kid was the football in this game. As Valerie finished up her phone conversation, Evan felt the urge to take strong moral action rise inside him.

Valerie slammed down the phone. "Thanks," she said to Evan. "I'm sorry to intrude."

"While we wait for the police to arrive," replied Evan, "I'll provide moral support."

"Moral support?" said Valerie in something close to a shriek. "What does that mean?"

"Your child has been abducted. I can't just stand by and let him be taken. I've heard of cases where kids got lost at shopping malls and some molester took them away, all because nobody was willing to do anything. That has to stop. People have to be willing to stand up and take action."

"I did do something. I called the cops. They'll take action."

Evan reflected on this for a couple of seconds. "It will take them a while to arrive. If we act right now, we can defuse the situation." He wasn't happy with the idea that some cop might steal his moment of glory, effectively erasing the credit that should accrue to him. The time for reflection passed; Evan strode to Jeff and Nancy's door and, without giving himself time to think, banged hard on it three times with his fist.

The bickering noises within stopped abruptly. Then came the incredulous roar of Jeff's voice: "What the hell do *you* want?"

"I want you to do what's right. Let the kid see his mother."

Nancy started to blare something, but it was covered up by Jeff's next salvo. "Man, stay the fuck out of my business!"

"Where it involves another human being, it's not just your business," admonished Evan. He was conscious of his increasing nervousness and tried to suppress it by talking. "It's not just a matter of the law. We all have moral responsibilities in this world. Consider the seeds you're planting in your child's personality that may sprout years down the line." Evan, emboldened by his own rhetoric, was gaining confidence. "The seeds of conflict are planted early. So are the seeds of depression and despair. Let's be reasonable. There's enough trouble in this world already – why are you adding to it?"

"What is this, New Age shit?" Jeff shot back.

"No, this is Old Age shit," said Evan, trying to get him to pay attention. "This is the wisdom of the ages."

"Excuse me, but what do you think you're doing?" said a sharp female voice behind Evan. He turned and saw Valerie. She flipped the hair out of her face and said, "I really don't think you're helping." She said this so fiercely that Evan felt flecks of spittle on his face.

"I'm providing moral support," said Evan. "How can you possibly object?"

"Just do me a favor and stay out of this."

"Why should I do that? Somebody has to stand up."

"Why do you think we called the cops?" said Valerie. The expression on her face was of puzzlement mixed with frustration, as if she were trying to decipher an urgent message in a language she barely knew. "They'll stand up. Now, thanks for letting me use your phone, but please stay out of the way."

Nancy's voice rang out behind the door. "Just go away, Valerie!"

Valerie's face turned red with rage. "Shut up and drink your vodka, Nancy!"

The two women traded insults. Jeff's voice added to the general din. Though he spoke loudly in a quavering, melodramatic tone, Evan couldn't make out what he was saying due to the noisy female chorus. Total irrationality seemed to be taking over. Evan backed off a few feet, in the direction of his apartment.

Isaiah, who lived down the hall, came out of his own apartment, releasing the odor of General Tso's chicken into the hallway. He surveyed the scene with a wary, watchful expression on his face, as if he were looking out for an intruder. He glanced at the overheating Valerie, then at Evan. "What's happening here?"

"I'm trying to defuse a domestic situation," said Evan.

Isaiah looked at him as if he had said he was trying to defuse a bomb. "Man, that is the stupidest thing. I don't know where you grew up, but you ever been in 'a domestic situation' before? People get crazy. Did anyone call the cops?"

"Yeah, I did. With a little help. But they're coming."

"If you're smart, you will get back inside." Isaiah retreated to his own apartment. Evan took his advice. As soon as he closed the door, he heard new noises, like heavy footsteps. He looked out through the peephole and saw that two policemen had arrived. The level of noise emanating from Jeff and Nancy's apartment dropped instantly.

The police, in stark contrast to Evan, managed to cool down the situation. He continued to watch as a fragile peace was enforced. It was as if Evan's intervention had achieved nothing at all. But reflecting on the situation, and on what Isaiah had said, he realized that he shouldn't have gotten involved in the first place. Still, the shrieks of the small child made him think there must be a better way to handle this.

Chapter 10.

Systemic Collapse

It was two o'clock in the afternoon and Woody Latour was dreaming of pancakes. The cakes were right in front of him, practically in his face, and he was dexterously wielding knife and fork. Fluffy buttermilk pancakes with maple syrup. Bacon on the side: dark, crispy and dry, as lean as possible. A big ceramic cup of French roast coffee. As Woody gorged himself on the pancakes, they renewed themselves – as soon as one stack disappeared into his stomach, a new stack appeared from nowhere, as if by magic, on the table in front of him. The buttermilk pancakes vanished, and were instantly replaced by a stack of chocolate-chip cakes topped with blueberries. His coffee cup magically refilled itself, this time with Sumatra, and Woody got to work on this continuation of the feast.

A waitress appeared out of nowhere and started yelling at him. Woody woke up. His phone was ringing. With groggy slowness, he picked it up.

"Woody!" said Mike. He sounded exasperated. "Can you come to the conference room? We've got a meeting now."

"Certainly, Michael. Just give me a second." What was it this time? As Woody hauled himself out of the chair, he made a mental note to have breakfast at his favorite diner the next day. He licked his lips and was disappointed not to taste syrup. Just before going to the conference room, he thought: Wait a minute, I don't know how long I'll be in that meeting; best to make a stop in the gentlemen's room.

After doing his business, he glided over to the sink. The little soap dispenser caught his attention in a way it had never done before. For the first time, he noticed that it looked like a metal bird with a long beak. He had seen it a million times, but somehow its bird-like appearance had never penetrated his mind in any conscious way. This tiny revelation inspired him to have fun with it. He put his hand on the bird's head and pumped the soap out vigorously, as if inflating a bicycle tire. By doing this, he got vastly more soap than he needed for hand-washing purposes. He worked the soap into a giant fluffy mass of suds with the aid of water. The fluffy suds resembled clouds, a fitting environment for the bird to fly through. Woody regarded the nature tableau which he had just created with pleasure and satisfaction. After performing his ablutions, he left the restroom. He did not shut off the water completely, but left a tiny trickle running into the slowly shrinking mass of suds. This stream completed the scene of nature, giving it a sense of life and motion. Woody could only hope that future visitors to the bathroom would appreciate what he had created.

When Woody finally entered the conference room, he found Eric and Mike engaged in a contentious exchange.

"*Solaris?*" said Mike.

"No. It's his other sci-fi film. There isn't a little girl in *Solaris*. Admit it – you haven't seen either film."

"I'm not prepared to admit that. There are some films we don't remember actually seeing, but bits of them lodge in our memory, which means I can't guarantee I have or haven't seen them. But what is the little girl doing?"

"She's got her head down on the table, and she's moving the glasses across the table using telepathy."

"Alright. I'll never get this one."

"*Stalker,*" said Eric. "It's the last shot. No points for you. Oh, hello there, Woody!"

"And a good day to you, gents," said Woody as he gradually eased himself into the chair at the head of the table. "So, Mike … you've called us together for a little meeting, eh?"

Mike looked uncomprehendingly at Woody. "Actually Woody… you're the one who scheduled this meeting."

"Really, is that so?" said Woody. He seemed genuinely puzzled for a second, then recovered. "Well that's fascinating. That means there was something I wanted to discuss."

Should I laugh at this? thought Eric. Mike started fiddling with his pen, flipping it around and bouncing it off the table.

"What could it be?" mused Woody. He gazed into the distance, then blurted: "Ah, yes. I remember now!"

"Well that's good," said Mike with some relief in his voice. "I thought you might be losing it in your old age!"

"Oh, I'm not *that* old, you know," gushed Woody, "but since you mentioned age, you made me feel a bit nostalgic. You gents might have noticed that it's a bit cold in this office. I've got a bit more padding than both of you, but even I am feeling it a little. And you know, that brings me back, to the time when I was in boarding school. As I recall, it was a rather cold day…"

"Oh, hey there Woody," blurted out Mike with just a hint of alarm in his voice. "I remember the last time you told me the story. It was funny. I was glad to hear it at that time."

Woody didn't take the hint. "We lived in dormitories in those days. The young people nowadays, they don't know how lucky they are. They've got central heating, central air conditioning, central plumbing, central refrigeration, central coffee, central anything you could wish for. But we young scholars, we only had *space heaters*. And would you believe it, they *charged* us to use those space heaters. We had our quarters piled up in little stacks next to our bed, don't you know, just to feed them to the space heaters. And woe betide the boy who did not carefully guard his stack of quarters..."

Woody rambled on. Eric was morbidly curious as to what other terrible hardships Woody was going to mention. Had he been subjected to outhouses on freezing nights, or cold oatmeal for breakfast? Yet Eric knew that there was no point in trying to follow Woody's story. He had tried to follow these stories in the past, and in every case, when the story ended, he always found himself in a remote and lonely place that had no connection to the way the story had started. And he couldn't even remember the steps by which he had arrived in that remote and lonely place. Woody was like a driver who set out to a particular destination, but took so many detours and changed his mind so many times that he ended up as far from his intended goal as possible. It was like someone trying to drive from Chicago to Milwaukee, and winding up in a remote village on the Canadian border, wondering how he had gotten there.

"... but you see, when we actually visited the building, we noticed a peculiar stench. Well, I looked into it, and I discovered that this place they were trying to foist on us as a 'renovated luxury apartment' had actually once been a stable to keep horses! Imagine my surprise! Lord only knows what kind of diseases might be lurking in a space like that."

Mike looked at his watch ostentatiously. "I'm sorry to interrupt, Woody, but I've got another commitment soon. Now, could we please get down to business? What was it you called us together for?"

"Oh of course! I almost forgot. Now, what was it? Oh yes, Curriculum 21."

"Huh?" said Eric involuntarily.

"Yes – I wanted to discuss Curriculum 21. That's the subject. That is why we are gathered here today."

Mike couldn't help looking disgusted. "Curriculum 21 is what we do here all day, every day. It's what we talk about, think about, moan about, all the time. And if we keep going at this rate, it's going to turn into Curriculum 22, or Curriculum Never."

"Curriculum 3000!" boomed Woody, raising his hands theatrically.

Mike ignored this attempt at deflection. "Just saying 'Curriculum 21' tells me nothing useful. Please, Woody, *can* you be more specific? Help us out here. What aspect of Curriculum 21, *specifically*, is bothering you today?"

"Very well," said Woody, suddenly decisive and business-like. "Looking over some of our recent material, it struck me that some essential elements are missing. Missing, or not implemented quite as they should be." He launched into a series of criticisms of the material they had been working on lately. According to Woody, not enough attention was being paid to practical concerns; the teaching material for the lower grades was too focused on grammar, the vocabulary was too advanced and not suitable for all potential markets, and some of the illustrations were not clear enough.

Eric and Mike listened to Woody with surprise and relief. His criticisms made sense. He had actually read the material and thought about it. He stuck to the point. It was like the clearing of a cloudy sky, with the sunshine causing all objects to stand out sharply in the environment. The old Woody was back, doing what he had been hired to do.

But the sun didn't stay out long; the clouds gathered, and the old Woody was suddenly occluded. "That brings me to a small point. Well, maybe it's small for *you two*, but I have to bring it up. It's one of the most important things in the teaching material, and both of you are ignoring it."

"Really. I wonder what it is," deadpanned Mike.

Woody said, putting big spaces between the words: "Systems – of – meaning!"

"Oh please. Not again."

Woody threw up his hands in despair. "Before you dismiss it, let me say this. We're not going to put together a curriculum with 'the blue book is on the table.' Or 'the quick brown fox jumped over the lazy dog.' No sir. Am I right, Eric?"

"Yeah, you're right. But we're missing something. If we want to incorporate the systems of meaning into the material, we'll need some sort of comprehensive presentation. You know, all the systems and how they function. Right now I can only remember a couple of these systems of meaning you refer to. It's hard to write material when you don't have much to go on."

Woody looked exasperated. "Gentlemen, you have numerous examples at your disposal. Do I really have to walk you through it? Well, I won't do it."

Having stated that he wouldn't do it, this is exactly what Woody did. "Remember, there is no such thing as a synonym. When I say 'Arthur arrived at the airport,' that means his plane landed. But when I say 'Arthur got to the airport,' that means he took a cab."

"How about 'Arthur went to the airport'?" asked Eric.

119

"Well *that's* completely different. Obviously, Arthur has only just set out, probably in his own car. We don't know if he has actually arrived there yet."

"But Woody," said Mike, "you just said that if he *arrived*, that means his plane has landed."

"I think your system needs a little more refinement," said Eric gently.

Woody looked flustered. "You two are not seeing the big picture. Of course we can tinker with the system, refine it as you say, but the point is, it has to be reflected in the final product."

"I like your earlier point about practical concerns," said Eric. "I agree that we should focus more on that."

Eric was trying to calm Woody down, but it didn't work. Woody starting huffing and puffing. "Look here, these things are not mutually exclusive! *Of course* those practical concerns need to be addressed. But one way we address them is by incorporating the *systems of meaning*. The systems of meaning *are* a practical concern! What's more practical than standing up? Do I have to illustrate it for you fellows?" Woody started jiggling his arms spasmodically, as if he were getting ready to blast off into space. His voice rose in volume and pitch. "Look! I'm sitting! I'm sitting in the chair. Sitting pretty. A sitting duck, if you please. And now, watch what I'm doing." He pushed on the armrests, wheezing as he did so. "I'm standing up." His body began to rise, slowly and jerkily; he pushed harder. "I'm standing up," he puffed. His face was becoming unusually red. As Mike and Eric watched with growing alarm, Woody's arms managed to push the rest of him free of the chair. For a moment Eric had a mental image of a forklift truck straining to hoist an oversized load. "I'm...standing *up*." He struggled to raise his shoulders and then his head, pushing the chair backwards as he did so. "I'm standing..."

"Take it easy, Woody!" said Mike.

amazon.com®

SNzVhfp6y6

Remit To:

Amazon.com
PO Box 80367
Seattle, WA 98108-80387
USA

Vendor Return
Shipment ID: 8800300240551
VRET ID: VRET7111307289531
RA #: 9L6OO-22112717ZQ-IGQ1-1
Process Date: November 27, 2022
LOG: Amazon.com

Shipped From:
2201 W 159TH ST
HARVEY , IL 60428-4804
United States

Shipping Address
zachary thaxton
3650 debby ln
franksville, WI 53126
United States

Amazon.com Vendor Return -- OVERSTOCK (RA #: 9L6OO-22112717ZQ-IGQ1-1)

Qty.	Item	ASIN	UPC/EAN
	SINGLE-PACKAGE SHIPMENT		
1	Abandon All Hope	X003AIKRGR	9781736827826

0/NzVhfp6y6/-1 of 1-//MKE5-NIT/vendor-returns/0/1205-15:00/0103-16:39 Pack Type : Smartpac
VRET**8800300240551

"I'm *standing*," Woody wheezed. His eyes went blank, his breaths were short and labored. "I'm – *stand* – "

Woody's eyes closed, his body went slack, and he hit the floor with a resounding thud. On the way down, he bumped against the chair, sending it reeling back into the wall, which it slammed into with a loud crack. "Oh my God!" came a shrill female voice from outside the conference room, where a couple of passers-by saw the action transpire through the room's glass wall. Mike and Eric both jumped up. Mike dashed out of the room and shouted "Call 911!" to no one in particular. Eric hovered around Woody's supine figure, wondering what to do. Many years before, he'd passed a first aid course, but now he couldn't remember anything he had learned. Maybe try artificial resuscitation? But Woody appeared to be still breathing, so that wasn't necessary. This meant he wouldn't have to clamp his mouth onto Woody's, which was a relief.

Things were so chaotic that Eric couldn't follow what was going on. Mike had disappeared. Eldritch employees crowded the door to the conference room, gawking at the spectacle of Woody Latour lying flat on the floor like a great fish laid out on a slab at an open-air market. Some gung-ho individual had brought a fire extinguisher with him. Eric wanted to point out that hosing Woody with the extinguisher probably wouldn't help any, but then realized that the guy had simply misread the nature of the emergency. Feeling that he should do something – anything – Eric picked up a small cushion from one of the office chairs and propped Woody's head on it. The head emitted a faint moan.

Eric saw a reason to take charge. "Can you all move out of the way, please? The paramedics are coming through soon." The crowd began to disperse. After a few minutes Mike came back, followed by a couple of medical personnel wheeling a gurney. Eric was amazed by the speed of the paramedics' response. He now had an excuse to get out of the way; with relief, he left the office to the paramedics and joined the rest of the employees out in cubicle land. The paramedics got busy. He heard them giving instructions and information, accompanied by the snap and clink of equipment being deployed. Now this is a real job, thought Eric; no nonsense about Curriculum 2000, Curriculum 21, Curriculum 3000, endless delays, pouting egos, decisions we'll make tomorrow, what the boss wants, or conflicting visions. This is *saving lives*, dammit!

The paramedics, summoning all their strength, successfully hoisted Woody onto the gurney and secured him in place. As they wheeled him out of the conference room, he was beginning to revive. His breathing was heavier as he gulped the air hungrily, and his moaning was turning into words, or at least fragments of words. "Where... wha... go... going... what hap... how..." Eric watched as the distressed cargo was pushed out of sight. He and Mike stood there, silently staring, as the other employees gradually went back to work. Mike turned to Eric and gave him a look that seemed to ask: What now?

They went back into the conference room to survey the damage. Coffee had spilled onto the table and the floor, presumably while the paramedics were doing their work. The chair wasn't damaged, but the wall was scuffed where the chair had hit it. Something dark and shiny was lying on the floor. Eric was startled when he caught sight of it: was it a small animal? But it wasn't breathing, moving or making any sound. He looked closer and realized that it was Woody Latour's hairpiece, which must have slid off while the paramedics were working on him.

They gathered their office detritus – notebooks, pens, the coffee cup, and Woody's hairpiece – and left the conference room. Mike said, "Maybe we should take the rest of the day off."

•

The stylus skated over the pliant, yielding vinyl as Eric collapsed on his sofa. The plangent drone of the English horn started up against a misty background of tape hiss. Eric had been lucky enough to find a high-quality British EMI pressing of Mahler's *Rückert Lieder* in good condition, much to be preferred to the mushy Angel pressing released in the United States.

Janet Baker's voice sounded almost disembodied as it rose up from the cushion of dark strings. *"Ich bin der Welt..."* she didn't quite sing the words as float them out into the air. Nineteen oh whenever this dated from. In Mahler's Vienna historical forces were crushing the old life like a juggernaut: psychoanalysis, twelve-tone music, and harsh functional architecture were blooming on the landscape like hallucinogenic mushrooms. The world-altering slaughter of World War I was only a few years away. Empires were on the verge of collapse. Yet the artist was able to step outside of it all, hovering in a private cocoon above the turmoil:

"Ich bin der Welt abhanden gekommen,
Mit der ich sonst viele Zeit verdorben..."

"I am lost to the world, where I wasted so much time... I live alone, in my heaven, in my love, in my song." Only six minutes of music, but it helped him to put the day's craziness behind him. Eric didn't want to think about Woody Latour's collapse, or about what was going on at Eldritch in general. That could all be dealt with later. He just wanted to stay in his heaven for a while like Mahler, in meditative solitude, and restore his equilibrium.

This private heaven was shattered by the ringing of the phone. It was Alina. They had made some plans for the following evening. "Oh, *hi*," said Eric, trying to express enthusiasm; he was not in the mood to talk right at this moment. "What's up?"

"Oh, I'm not feeling well." She giggled slightly.

"That's too bad." *Damn!* He knew exactly what she was going to say next.

"So, I'm afraid I can't make it tomorrow night. Maybe when I will feel better?"

"Yeah. I hope so. What's wrong?"

She had a cold, or some such all-purpose illness. Eric heard her out and offered some trite words of comfort, then hung up. A void had opened where tomorrow night's events were supposed to be. On reflection, he decided it would be better if they didn't meet tomorrow. He needed to stay in his cocoon for a few days.

•

When Mike and Eric came to work the next day, they were informed by email that Audrey Shroom wished to see them at once. Dutifully, they trooped up to the third and top floor of the building.

Audrey was seated at her desk. This was the first time Eric had ever been in her office, so he took a good look around. On the wall behind the desk, hung in a place where you couldn't miss it, was Audrey's MBA diploma from Northwestern. A bookshelf in the corner was about half-filled with books. Most of them had to do with business or management, although Eric noticed a number of inspirational and self-help volumes, including such hits of the genre as *All I Really Need to Know I Learned in Kindergarten* and *The 7 Habits of Highly Effective People.* It reminded him disturbingly of Porter and Nora's home in Glenview, but the number of such books was much smaller here in the office. A small stack of magazines

(with *The Economist* on top) sat perfectly placed in the
middle of the desk; they looked freshly delivered, and
were probably yet unread. The neatness and cleanliness
of everything made Eric feel slightly ashamed of his own
humble cubicle, with its detritus and the Dante quote
stuck on the partition. He got the sense that Audrey
would not tolerate such sloppiness and cynicism in her
own space. Audrey herself wore a dignified and sober
brown suit; her dark shoulder-length hair framed her
round, pensive face.

She drummed her fingers on the desk for a few seconds before speaking. "In view of yesterday's unfortunate event, you Michael Riordan are now the acting head
of the Curriculum Development Department. You Eric
Freeman will continue working in the same capacity as
before, but this makes you effectively the number two
person in the department now. Consider it an informal
promotion. We may formalize it at a later stage, depend-
ing on how it goes."

"Any news of Woody?" asked Eric.

"Heart attack is what they're saying. He is resting in
the hospital now. I can't tell you any more at this time.
We have no idea how long he will be out of commission.
When we get an update on his condition, that will give us
some clarity. I can't confirm that this is a promotion yet,
officially. But for now – you're the boss, Mike. Curriculum Development depends on you." Audrey appeared not
to know that, in reality, Curriculum Development had
depended on Mike for a long time already – he had been
the acting head of the department for a while, in a sense,
so the sensation of being the boss was not an entirely new
one for him.

"We have another issue," said Mike. "We're getting
a bit short-handed now. We've got our IT guy and our
administrative assistants, but with Woody out of the

picture, I think we're going to need a third person here. Fairly soon."

"I sympathize," said Audrey. "We'll have to look into that. What about all these people who answered your ad? Do any of them seem like suitable candidates?"

"No," said Eric. "Maybe. I don't know."

"Ditto," said Mike. "But they applied for temporary, short-term jobs. This is a different situation. If we put out an advertisement for a new full-time position, we might get more suitable responses."

"We'll look into it," said Audrey. "Until we can budget for a new full-time position, we'll have to continue and even expand the use of independent contractors."

"We're still working through the big pile of responses that we got," said Eric. "One of these days, I hope to strike gold. Or at least, some other useful metal."

Chapter 11.

Don Quixote on the Roof

"The bathroom's in here," said Eric. "Sorry about the mess."

"No worries," said Evan. "I live in a messy apartment myself." Eric had manifested politeness and respect for his guest today by cleaning the bathroom thoroughly; however, the rest of the apartment was in its usual state.

Eric brought the fill valve, still in its box from the hardware store, to the bathroom and let Evan get to work. "The water never completely shuts off after I flush it. The guy at the hardware store told me that these valves tend to fill up with sand from Lake Michigan, and that you should replace them every few years. Well, I'd rather let someone else do the replacing."

"Ever since the snow melted, I've been expanding my repertoire. Toilets are just one of the things I fix." Evan took the lid off the toilet tank, and surveyed the inside.

"You wanna go out and get some lunch after this?" asked Eric. "My treat. In addition to whatever fee you charge."

"Sounds good, thanks."

•

"Is it mostly the handyman stuff keeping you together?" asked Eric, munching his sandwich.

"I do office jobs as well," said Evan. "Through a temp agency. But I can't count on them exclusively."

"I'm glad I kept your card," said Eric. "I got sick of hearing that hissing sound – no matter how many times I would flush, the water wouldn't stop running – so I called you." They were at one of Eric's local hangouts, a coffee house located under the El line. It was a homey venue decorated with all kinds of household junk (old editions of books, cooking implements that hadn't been used in generations), and it boasted amateurish drawings and photographs done by the staff, who seemed to consist mostly of aspiring artists and functional layabouts. Occasionally you could hear the rumble of a train overhead, which added to the ramshackle atmosphere. Eric liked the vibe of the place: it reminded him of his own apartment, but with service.

"I appreciate this," said Evan. He was digging into a Ciabatta Whatever, the café's name for this particular sandwich, called such in honor of the younger generation's current favorite word, with a raspberry latte on the side. "I don't usually go out to eat, and I'm not much of a cook."

"How's the plan to save the world going?"

"I've had a couple of setbacks. But I can't let myself get disheartened. A wise man said that a journey of a thousand miles must begin with a single step. He forgot to say that you might step in mud. But he was still right."

"I gotta say," said Eric, "you weren't the only person I could have called to fix the toilet. But you are probably more interesting to talk to than any of them. I don't know a lot of handymen who are writing philosophical treatises."

"Thanks for the compliment. If I'm not interesting, then I'm nothing."

"That's harsh. What setbacks have you experienced?"

Evan told him about his recent work adventures, and his intervention attempt with his dysfunctional neighbors. Eric pointed out the bright side. "You did get them to pay the temps for the work they did. That's not nothing."

"It's a start. It also relates to the chapter I'm writing in *The Positive Life*, on the value of altruism. I realized that you never do anything just for other people. You do everything for yourself, and it might have a knock-on effect that benefits others. Think about it – I did this thing for you, not because I wanted to benefit you, but because I want to feel that I am a good person. But you benefited from it. People in the helping professions all have this mentality."

"That sounds like a psychological version of Adam Smith's 'invisible hand' argument."

Evan looked at Eric blankly. "Adam who?"

Another haphazardly educated college dropout, thought Eric. He took the opportunity to deadpan. "He was the lead singer for the band Adam and the Ants. He had this theory that, if one of your hands was invisible, then that means … oh what the hell, I've forgotten the details. You don't need to know it anyway. But you know who you remind me of? Don Quixote!" said Eric.

"Don who?"

"Don Quixote was a guy I used to work with," said Eric. He watched Evan's face for any sign that Evan knew he was joking, but the face remained serious and attentive. Funny, he thought; even millions of people who hadn't read the book knew who the Don was – the addled old man who fantasized he was a knight and set out to right the world's wrongs was a familiar archetype. But Evan looked like he had honestly never heard of him. Eric decided that now would be a good time for a bathroom break. He excused himself, leaving Evan to finish his raspberry latte and get himself a glass of water.

A few minutes later, Eric was back to continue the story. "Don Quixote was the head of our department before Woody was hired. Don started out normally, but I think he got bored with his work after a while. He started watching movies about superheroes, reading comic books, and stuff like that. You know, they call comic books 'graphic novels' nowadays and that's supposed to make them more serious, but they have the same effect on people. For some reason, Don got the idea into his head that he should be a superhero or comic book hero himself. But when you work for a company like Eldritch…the corporate culture doesn't allow you a lot of space to realize your dreams."

"So what happened?"

"One day, Don became convinced that extraterrestrials had landed on the roof of our office building. He sent an e-mail to everyone warning of the danger. He said he was going to do something about it. Then he went up to the roof, intending to save us from this threat. Some employees were outside at the time. They saw him raving and shouting, but they couldn't make out what he was saying. He was waving a broom around as if it were some kind of weapon. After a while, the cops came and took him away."

"That's very weird. Didn't anyone notice that something was wrong with him before he went up on the roof?"

"A few people had their concerns. But in a place like Eldritch, where people tend to stick to their cubicles and departments and don't interact much, nobody wanted to intervene. There was one exception. Don had a friend in the IT department, a guy named Sancho Panza. A Mexican

130

dude, from Berwyn. Sancho was the opposite of Don. He thought Don's ideas about being a superhero were nuts. Sancho was a guy with no illusions and no grand plans. He just wanted to get his job done, then go home and enjoy life. Family, church, work and his hobbies were more than enough for him. He tried to cure Don's delusions, but sadly, it was too late."

"Maybe Sancho should have become the department head."

"That would have been logical, so of course nobody considered it. But I doubt that Sancho would have wanted the job. Too much responsibility, too much worry." Eric smiled. "Anyway, we got Woody Latour, and he's a monster of efficiency and good sense compared to Don."

"So why do you say that I'm like Don?" asked Evan.

"Well, you..." Eric paused. He couldn't say that Evan was delusional like Don Quixote, or naïve, or had an unjustifiable sense of his own righteousness, and of course he couldn't say he was crazy like the Don. He came out with: "Both you and Don Quixote have a strong sense of how you'd like the world to be, and you both try very hard to change it. You're both, in that sense, idealists."

"Maybe. I'm not planning to go up on the roof and wave a broom around."

Eric slammed down his coffee cup and stared hard at Evan. "I have a confession to make. That story I just told you? It was all bullshit. I made it up. Our department head was never called Don Quixote, and he never went crazy like that. I stole the story from a 17th-century Spanish novel – a classic – and I transposed it to my present life."

With a sly smile, Evan said: "I thought that's what you were doing. But I didn't say anything, because I wanted to see how it would end."

"Have you read the book?"

"No. But I've heard of it. You must have read it. Did Don Quixote succeed in changing the world?"

"Well, to tell the truth, it's been a long time since I read it... I don't really remember. Maybe you should read it for yourself."

Evan's face grew serious again. "Oh, no. I prefer not to read novels."

"Why is that?"

"They are works of fantasy. Every novel ever written is simply a pack of lies." He said this confidently but without anger, so that it sounded like part of a credo. "I'm aware that I should read more. In college, I got in trouble with my professors because I preferred to think for myself rather than read the books they assigned me. Now, I realize there are big gaps in my knowledge. I should read philosophy, psychology, history. But I avoid fiction. If I want to understand the real world, I need books that deal with it directly."

"Wow, that's harsh. Do you watch movies?"

"Only documentaries."

"Music?"

"Haven't made up my mind about that. But I'm not that interested in music anyway, so it's not a major temptation. The development of an aesthetic sense is detrimental to the mind of a person of action such as myself. It causes me to take pleasure in the world as it is or was, and thus hobbles my motivation to change the world into something better."

"Don't you ever just want to relax with a bag of chips and watch *The Simpsons*?"

"I don't have a TV."

"That's the way to avoid temptation."

"In fact, I'm not tempted by it," said Evan. "I've stopped wasting my time on these frivolities. You can put a bigscreen TV in my room and I will never turn it on. I made a decision and I followed it through."

One last probe on Eric's part: "What about, you know – relationships, friends, that sort of thing?"

"There was a girl I sort of liked back when I was at Eastbrook. But I didn't stay there long, and anyway, when I got to know her a little more, I realized she was shallow. All that human stuff is temporarily on hold. I have to establish myself first."

It looks like the suburbs have bred an undereducated, ascetic Gnostic philosopher who rejects the things of this world and wants to show us the path of righteousness, thought Eric. "When is *The Positive Life* going to be finished? Do I get to read it?"

"I hope by the end of this year. It all depends on how well my experiment in living goes. When it's finished, everyone will get to read it."

Chapter 12.

Condemned to Davenport

Entering his apartment a few days later, Eric was greeted by the blinking light of his answering machine, indicating that he had a message. It was from his sister Nora. "Hi Eric. Just wanted to ask if you're free to come to a little house party at our place this Saturday. I can pick you up at the Metra and drop you off after. Feel free to bring a friend. Let us know if you can make it!"

Eric hadn't seen them for a few months, and he had nothing else to do on Saturday, so he decided to go. He was intrigued by the permission to "bring a friend." During his most recent phone conversation with Mom, he had dropped the news that he was sort of going out, sort of not (he wasn't even sure himself), with Alina. It appeared that this piece of information had been conveyed to the Hotchkisses. This party would give him a chance to show them that he was making something like a commitment, or that he was able to think of making something like a commitment, for a while at least, or more generally, that he was capable of moving beyond his own selfish interests. Or something like that.

Glenview was a pleasant place to visit because, unlike the suburbs to the northwest of the city that Eric traversed on his daily commute, it was a traditional town, with sidewalks, houses that looked different from each other and not like identical industrial products rolling off an assembly line, and an old-fashioned (if somewhat sleepy and underutilized) downtown. Porter and Nora lived in one of these traditional houses, with a traditional sidewalk in front of it.

On Saturday, Nora met them at the train station, and then drove them to the house. When they arrived, Eric saw a Shetland sheepdog tethered in the yard to a long cord. The dog perked up its long pointy ears, barked, and ran towards them. "Hey, Waldick!" Eric exclaimed, as the dog raised its paws and howled in greeting.

"Hi, doggie," said Alina.

Eric was proud of the fact that the dog was named Waldick, because it was the only sign that he had ever influenced Nora and Porter in any way. The name derived from a story he had told them a few years before, and which he had read in one of those compendiums of amusing and interesting facts that one can typically find in the humor section of a bookstore. The Brazilian pop singer Waldick Soriano was giving a concert, singing his big hit *"Eu não sou cachorro, não"* ("I am not a dog, no"), when a dog emerged from the wings, wearing a sign that said "I am not Waldick Soriano." Instead of taking this humorous interjection in stride, Soriano was miffed and offended. He started insulting the audience, then walked off, leaving the stage to the dog. Something like a riot followed Soriano's hissy fit, although the account in the book was hazy on the details.

But Eric always remembered the story, and when he told it to Porter and Nora, they laughed. Nora found it so funny that she insisted if they ever got a dog, it would be called Waldick. One day, shortly thereafter, they did get a dog. Porter objected to the name Waldick, but his resistance was feeble, and Nora's insistence on the name prevailed. The dog was indeed given the name Waldick. Yet Porter never completely reconciled himself to the name; he resented the idea of having to explain to neighbors whom he met when walking the dog how it had acquired such an odd name. He told neighbors and other outsiders that the dog was called Sparky. But in the house, among relatives and close friends, the dog was always called by his official name. Eric took a sneaky pride in the whole situation, not just because he had managed to influence them, but also because he had thereby created a tiny rift in their oh-so-perfect suburban marriage.

"Thank you for the drive," said Alina.

"No problem," said Nora as they walked up to the front door. The words "One Sixty Three" were displayed on it in golden curlicue letters.

"I smell something," said Eric.

"Porter's in the backyard, cooking burgers," said Nora. Although it would have been easy to walk around the house to get to the backyard, Nora steered them through the interior.

One of the things Eric appreciated, either when he was apartment-hunting or when he was visiting people's homes, was the chance to get a peek into the lives of other people, and in that way to acquire a sense of the diversity of the human experience. After a while, it was easy to put the inhabitants into slots. He had, for instance, encountered the following types over the years: The Intellectual (books everywhere on a variety of topics, functional furniture, messy); The Cheerful Philistine (no books at all, but a huge TV set and a copy of *People* magazine on the very clean glass coffee table); The Pop Culture Junkie (pictures of currently fashionable pop musicians and movie stars on the walls, no publications older than the current year); The Sports Fanatic (posters of a particular sports team, as well as such memorabilia as signed baseballs and saved tickets from particularly memorable games); The Religious Zealot (objects pertaining to a particular religion hung on the walls, and books relating to that religion on the shelves, with a notable paucity of books on other subjects); The Political Zealot (objects pertaining to a particular political movement or party hung on the walls, and books relating to that political movement or party on the shelves, with a notable paucity of books on other subjects); The Identity-Based Self-Obsessive (obsessed with his or her ethnic and/or racial heritage and/or sexual orientation and/or other identity category, with objects ranging from kitsch of the leprechauns-and-shamrocks type to serious works of art, plus a whole shelf of books on the subject of his or her identity category); and The Slob (a random mess of objects piled up over the years, suggesting that their possessor was not specifically interested in anything, and particularly not interested in keeping the place clean). The list of possible permutations, gradations, and combinations of these types was as endless as the human race. Eric did not exempt himself from scrutiny, and recognized that he combined aspects of The Intellectual and The Slob.

Some time had passed since Eric was last at Porter and Nora's house, and taking a fresh view as he trained his sociological eye on its contents, he classified them as The Respectable Professional Suburban Couple. As he and Alina passed through the house, they took in the vacation photos on the wall (Italy, Mexico, Colorado – the last when visiting Mom), the educational toys for the kids (solid geometrical wooden blocks, a toy musical keyboard), the self-help and management books on the shelves, the copies of *Vogue*,

Time and the local suburban newspaper on the coffee table, the big fluffy blue sofa, and the black, flat television. "Excuse the mess," said Nora, even though the house wasn't noticeably messy – in fact, it was about a hundred times cleaner than Eric's apartment. "We need to clean this place up."

"Mommy! Mommy!" screamed Lianna from outside. She was sprawled on the grass, playing with some sort of expanding and contracting red goo, molding it into shapes and then pulling them into other shapes. This was presumably another educational toy, intended to teach kids mastery of the ever-changing, ever-flowing spatial world. Porter stood at the grill, flipping burgers. When he saw Eric and Alina, he dropped the spatula, ran over to them and said hello.

"Where's Brent?" Nora asked him.

"Playing soccer," said Porter. "I have to pick him up at four." He looked somewhat fatter than when Eric had last seen him; his shirt and jeans didn't have much room to spare. Now that the warm weather was here, he couldn't hide his expansion under a layer of thick clothes.

There were a couple of neighbors milling about in the back yard, people whom Eric had never met. He exchanged pleasantries with them, and then started looking around for any goodies that might be available, while waiting for Porter to finish cooking the burgers. Waldick the dog had been moved to the backyard, and Eric welcomed the opportunity to socialize with him. Since he was an apartment dweller, he couldn't have his own dog, and this was a source of regret. Meanwhile, Porter got a conversation going with Alina. "So, where are you from?" he asked.

"Moscow," said Alina.

"I hear it gets cold there."

"It does. Very cold sometimes. But then, it gets hot in summer." Alina didn't want Porter to think Moscow was always icy cold.

"It gets cold here, too," he remarked perceptively.

"Yes, I know." She smiled to show that their common experience of cold was a bond between them. "I was here all last winter."

"It hasn't been as cold here recently as it was in the eighties. Maybe there's something to this global warming business." He wished he hadn't said that; as a topic of conversation, global warming was a bit heavy for this kind of get-together.

Luckily, she didn't take the bait. "Maybe."

"I've never been to Russia," he said, "but I would like to go sometime. I'm sure there are a lot of interesting things to see." Porter was aware that some kind of cataclysmic change had taken place in Russia in the last ten years, but he wasn't entirely sure as to the nature of it. He got the uncomfortable feeling that he was wading into water that was too deep for him. "But, if it's colder there than it is here, maybe I shouldn't go!"

Lianna screamed again. Alina had mercy on Porter and shifted her attention to the small child. "How old is she?"

"Three." Lianna was becoming bored with her goo. She was stretching the substance out into long sinewy strings while droning over and over again "mommy, mommy" in as many different tones and pitches as she could, like a Baroque composer trying to get maximum utility out of the words *kyrie eleison*.

"This is Alina, Lianna," said Porter. "She's from Russia."

Lianna began to cry. She threw her goo onto the grass. The strained conversation fizzled out as Porter turned his attention to his crying child. "Hey Nora, can you help me out here?" Nora came over to soak up Lianna's attention so Porter could get back to grilling. Eric wandered away from the dog and toward the grill, in the process engaging Porter's attention. They began a banal conversation, opening with some pleasantries about work and the weather. This time, Porter talked about how warm it was getting. Eric saw a big bowl of cheese-flavored popcorn on the table in the backyard, and excused himse himself to fill up. Under the table was a cooler full of beer; he took advantage of that too.

When he returned, Porter was talking about child-rearing strategies with Alina, who appeared to be genuinely interested. "Nora, you know, has the kids listening to Mozart and Bach because it's supposed to be good for their brains. You know, those CDs with titles like *Baby Needs Bach*, *Baby Needs Mozart* and so on. I wish we could just give the kids a pill, it's easier than making them listen to an entire symphony by Bach."

Eric failed to stifle his inner pedant. "Actually, Bach didn't write any symphonies. In any case, I think this is just a fad; there's not a lot of research to back it up. You should listen to music because you like it, not because it might add half a point to your IQ if you listen to fugues and variations every day for a year."

"Well the kids seem to like it," said Porter.

"Problem solved, then," said Eric.

Eventually, as Eric went on happily stuffing himself, they wandered onto the topic of real estate. Porter began talking about which suburbs were becoming increasingly desirable; he sounded as if he had memorized the *Tribune*'s real estate section just for this occasion. He also talked about how much he and Nora enjoyed living in Glenview. Eric suspected that he was encouraged by Eric's apparent relationship with Alina, and was already positioning himself as an informal real estate agent for the inevitable time when Eric would "form a family" and decide to move out of the big city. Either that, or he just liked talking about real estate.

At one point, Porter slurped his beer noisily, then announced, "I don't know why you're still living in the city."

"Why shouldn't I?" said Eric.

"Well, it's been a while since I was there. For good reason, I can tell you. You know, the last time I was there, I had to drive through the South Side to get where I was going, and wouldn't you know it, there was a detour..."

Eric knew what was coming. The suburbanite's ride through Hell. He'd heard variations on this story more times than he could count. He used to tell it himself, back in the old days. Instead of trying to follow Porter's narrative, he decided to count the clichés, the tropes of the story, as they came marching out of Porter's mouth. Sure enough, there was the "war zone," then came "looked like it had been bombed," "gang graffiti," "sitting on the front stoop drinking malt liquor," "big baggy shorts," "gold chains," "sweating bullets," "what do these people do all day?", "sure glad when the light turned green," and finally "not going back without a bullet-proof vest."

But when Eric tried to answer Porter's question about why he still lived in the city, he found himself resorting to equally well-worn clichés: "ethnic restaurants," "interesting stores," "live theater," "street festivals," "you can meet interesting people," "don't have to drive everywhere," "hip coffee shops," "the lake."

Porter waxed philosophical. "You know, in a certain sense, it really shouldn't matter where you live. Any place is going to be better if you make a commitment to it. If you say to yourself: 'This is going to be my home now.'"

"There's that dreaded word 'commitment'," said Eric. "I should have figured that's where you were going."

"Look at it this way," said Porter. "What if you were condemned to live the rest of your life in Davenport, Iowa? And you had to stay within the city limits, without ever having the possibility of getting out, for your whole life?"

"What's wrong with Davenport?"

"Nothing's wrong with Davenport. I hear it's pretty nice. But you're missing the point of the exercise."

"It's an exercise? What self-help book did you get it from?"

"None. You do know that self-help books are not the only thing I read, right?"

"I'll take your word for it. But what's the point of the exercise?"

"The point," continued Porter, "is that you will live life to the fullest when you accept circumstances you can't change. Like, maybe you won't find your ideal career in Davenport, and you have no choice but to make the absolute most of your opportunities in that non-ideal career. You know – you channel all your energies into it. And eventually, by a paradox, that career *becomes* the ideal one for you. Just because you had no choice."

"How about an arranged marriage? Do you think that'll make me happy? I guess my big mistake was not being born in a farming village in ancient Mesopotamia. The lack of opportunity would have made me the happiest guy in the world." Eric shoved his hand into the bowl of cheese-flavored popcorn and munched while he awaited Porter's answer.

"It's probably a good idea to restrict yourself to scenarios you may actually encounter in reality."

"Like being stuck in Davenport my whole life."

"No, I mean like finding yourself in a place or a job or a marriage you can't get out of. And then realizing you have to make the most of it. And that it's not the worst place to be."

"Porter, you live in a John Hughes movie. I think you like it, right? No Davenport for you. But I'll take it under advisement," said Eric. It was time to head out to the lawn, where Alina and Nora were chatting about recipes, and get himself one more beer. Just one more beer, and then I think it's time to leave, he decided.

●

"See, that's why I like Chicago," said Nora, as she was driving Eric and Alina back to the Metra station. "The driver slows down and lets me pass. It's not like New York where they run you over without hesitation."

"We're in the suburbs," said Eric.

"Indeed we are. And?"

"We're in the suburbs. Not in the city. Have you ever even been in the New York suburbs? They're suburbs like any others. Your comparison doesn't make sense."

"Well, aren't we being pedantic today."

"Sorry," said Eric. "Not feeling so great all of a sudden."

"You okay there, Eric?" asked Nora. "That's not a happy face you've got on."

"A little bit too much cheese popcorn. And I washed it down with beer."

"That doesn't sound good. Should we stop and get you some fizzy water?"

"No, I can't bear to think of drinking anything right now," Eric gasped.

"Anything else?" said Nora.

"I had some cake, and also a couple of burgers. I think one of the burgers was undercooked."

"No, I mean is there anything else we can do for you?"

"No."

"Here, have a mint," said Alina, trying to help.

"Don't worry, it'll get better." Eric turned to the window, watching life go by on Willow Road – normal life that, right at this moment, excluded him and his stomach. Cars whizzed past; looking at them only made him feel worse. Upscale housing developments with names like Plaza del Prado and Glastonbury Acres lined the road. Eric thought about how stupid these names were. He saw a couple of cyclists negotiating the traffic on the road, and he thought about how stupid the cyclists were.

"I'm glad *I* didn't touch the cheese-flavored popcorn!" said Nora.

At this mention of cheese-flavored popcorn, combined with the sight of cars coming from the opposite direction at an upsetting velocity, something turned over in Eric. It was as if a switch had been flipped in his stomach, releasing a sudden flow of energy. Then the window came down and Eric's head was sticking out of it. The explosive force generated in his stomach propelled a stream from his mouth, in yellow, brown and other colors, in liquid and in chunks, flying through the air like a filthy ribbon. Inside Eric's tormented head, various noises blended into a smothering roar as another savage force gathered inside him and ejected a further load through his open gullet. As the last of the stream of vomit exited his body, the world began to return to its normal dimensions. Nora was shouting something, but Eric couldn't yet make out what it was. The car jerked to the right, onto a side street. The roaring noise inside his head subsided, and he took a deep breath. The car stopped. With trepidation, he turned his head.

Nora was giving him a look – half-concerned, half-mocking. "You know, maybe you should have let me get you some fizzy water."

"Wouldn't help," he gasped.

"Well, I can't have you like this in the car. Let's find a convenience store."

Alina was silent. Eric could barely bring himself to glance toward her in the back seat. In the split second that he looked, she seemed to be smiling at the comedy of the situation. But he looked away before he could discern anything else in her expression.

They stopped at a gas station. Eric cleaned up in the bathroom and settled his stomach with a Coke. Then Nora drove them to the Metra station. On the train back into the city, Eric tried to crack a few jokes about the situation, but Alina didn't laugh as much as he wanted her to.

•

The next day, Eric knew he should call Alina, but he also dreaded doing it. He spent most of Sunday looking for reasons to avoid calling her. After stuffing himself with Indian food at the local buffet – the previous day's adventure had left a big gap in his stomach that needed to be filled – he spun a recent vinyl acquisition, *Muswell Hillbillies* by the Kinks. While listening to it, he drank a craft beer to get his courage up. Even though Eric was usually a pig, when it came to things that mattered, he showed the appropriate respect: he didn't drink the beer out of a bottle, but poured it into a clean, proper glass first. Listening, Eric realized that, just like Ray Davies, he was a twentieth-century man but he wasn't too happy about being one; however, he only had to wait a couple of years for a new century to begin. With that thought in mind, he took the Kinks album off the platter and replaced it with *In the Court of the Crimson King*. Surely it would be more fun to live as a 21st Century Schizoid Man than as a mere 20th Century Man? The instrumental blasts, distorted vocals, and grotesque imagery made the upcoming century sound even scarier than the present one. To make matters worse, the King Crimson album's overall theme of the decay and collapse of empires brought to mind Alina's earlier comments about societal fragility; the whole topic depressed him. Eric took the album off after the first track. He didn't want to live in the future, nor did he like the present very much, so – possibly influenced by the title of the Kinks album – he plopped a Smithsonian Folkways LP of Appalachian mountain songs, recorded decades earlier, onto the turntable. The rustic music evoked a distant, mysterious world, much farther away in spirit than the Kinks' loathing of the modern age and its bureaucratic tyranny, and he was able to lose himself in the crackly fiddles and banjos for a while, with their evocations of misty mountains, deep forests, and whiskey slowly maturing in oak casks. He continued to listen, drink, and burp up the aftertaste of Indian food, while a part of him was hoping that Alina would call him before he called her. That would at least be a good sign, implying that she wanted to stay in touch. But she didn't call, and as evening started to move in, Eric gave up on the distractions and dialed her number.

"Hi Eric." No sign of hesitation or withdrawal on her part. "Are you feeling better today?"

"Yes I am, thank you." This sounded too formal, so he tried a different approach. "In fact, I'm feeling great! Never better. Ready to dance the night away!" Now he realized that the cheerfulness sounded forced. He couldn't win either way, so on his third try he opted for neutrality. "No, seriously. I was bad for a while yesterday, but I'm better now."

"That's good to hear. Listen, I've been thinking and – "

"Thinking. Uh-oh."

"Yes, thinking. Maybe we should not see each other for a while."

"Oh...okay," said Eric. "Any particular reason? Or do you just need a break?"

"After yesterday, I am not sure if I like your behavior so much."

"So you don't want to see me anymore because you saw me vomiting in the car? People vomit all the time. I know it's not a pleasant thing to watch, but come on."

"Here's what I think," said Alina. "Vomit is a symbol of something larger than itself. There is good vomit and bad vomit. If you work to help people in a natural disaster, and you get tired and sick and you see dead bodies...then you can vomit. And it's good vomit because you worked for it. You can be proud of that vomit. But what you did, you ate all that bad food, and then in the car…that is bad vomit and I cannot justify it."

"Vomit is a symbol? Is that what they taught you at the Gorky Literary Institution or whatever that school is that you went to?"

"Forget it. You're obviously not listening to what I'm saying." Eric was silent, so she continued. "That is your whole problem. Not just about vomit. About everything." She let a few seconds pass, then said: "Steve did that."

"Uh…Steve?"

"Steve. My former husband. He vomited like that sometimes."

"Oh."

When they stopped talking, Eric felt relief. He could go back to his old, familiar, comfortable way of living. The Alina project had failed, but that was no surprise. He poured a bowl of Cocoa Puffs (cereal as a snack was one of his weaknesses), topped it with a sliced-up banana, put some Bruckner on the stereo (the Seventh Symphony), and plopped himself down on the sofa. Anton Bruckner lacked social skills and had poor dress sense; his interactions with women were the stuff of comedy. For this reason, Eric felt some sympathy with him. But Bruckner also composed cathedrals in sound that listeners were still inhabiting long after his death, and there was scant evidence that Eric could ever accomplish anything that impressive. He drove away that depressing thought and allowed the meditative music, with its imposing blocks of brass tone and winding string-driven melodies, to create a yogi-like order and detachment in his mind. Now, he just had to come up with a convincing breakup story for Porter and Mom, in case they should ask about it.

Chapter 13.

Crisis Management

One morning, Eric came in a little earlier than usual to find Mike already at his desk, staring at his computer screen. Eric waved hello and headed straight for his corner cubicle. He was impressed by Mike's work ethic and also a little shamed by it. Eldritch didn't officially have an "employee of the month" award, but if it did, Mike deserved to get it many times over. Mike was certainly making a lot more productive use of his time than Eric, who was always looking for excuses to indulge in long coffee and lunch breaks, as well as goofing off more generally.

Eric booted up, swallowed some strong coffee, and awaited work with his usual bored indifference. Various emails had come in; luckily, none of them required his immediate attention. He scanned the news briefly. The new European Central Bank was opening; a few thousand miles away,

Pakistan had just conducted a second nuclear test. Closer to home, Kenneth Starr was continuing his pursuit of the President; "that woman, Miss Lewinsky" had given handwriting and fingerprint samples to the FBI at Starr's request. No global or even local cataclysm was imminent, so he decided he might as well get some work done. He opened the chapter he was working on. This one introduced the delicate subject of bathrooms and other aspects of personal hygiene. The ladies' room was introduced – all right and good – but under it was a linguistic barbarism Eric had never seen before: "the gentlemen's room." This was obviously a leftover Woodyism, one which they hadn't corrected yet. It was typical Woody in its pretentious over-erudition. The sign on the bathroom door says "Gentlemen," but nobody refers to it as "the gentlemen's room." It's always "the men's room."

"Hey Mike. Have you ever, *ever* in your life, heard the men's room referred to as 'the gentlemen's room'?" Eric sipped some coffee, savoring the hazelnut flavor. "I mean, it's sad that Woody had his heart attack, but now we have to clean up the mess he made *by ourselves.* Do you think we should send this stuff to his hospital bed so he'll have some productive work to do? We can call it 'outsourcing,' and even have him registered in India, so it all looks modern and trendy."

Mike said nothing. Eric stood up and walked over to Mike's cubicle. Mike was still hunched over, staring at the screen. "Hey Mike?" No answer. "You up for a quick round of First Shot – Last Shot?" Eric nudged Mike on the shoulder. Mike's upper body fell forward and his head hit the computer keyboard with a crack. "Shit," said Eric.

He turned around and looked out at the floor, where employees were starting to arrive. "Hey. Can I get some help here? We've got, I don't know what, some kind of emergency."

149

"Omigod. Is he dead?" said a plump young woman.

Eric poked Mike's back. "Hey Mike, buddy, wake up," he said. Nothing happened.

"Dead? Who's dead?" came a booming male voice, somewhere behind the woman. People moved in a quick, disorganized rush towards Mike's slumped body, still perched in the ergonomic office chair. "Omigod you're right." "He's dead!" "Are you sure?" "Omigod call a doctor." "But he's dead!" "Are you sure?" "Call someone!"

●

"It's like this department has a curse on it," said Eric. He was sitting in Audrey Shroom's office.

"This must be a real shock to you," said Audrey. She looked deflated. She spoke more softly and slowly than usual. "Apparently he was sitting there all night. Time of death will be hard to establish. He had a reputation for being a hard worker, so nobody was surprised to see him there. He might be working late and coming in early. His wife and daughter went out of town for a couple of days, so nobody called to ask about him." The phone rang, but she let it go to her voicemail. "I used to do tech support in a major law firm downtown. You wouldn't believe the macho work ethic they had. All the associates were trying to make partner. None of them wanted to get a reputation as the first to go home. So they stuck it out, often past midnight. If they wanted to leave before ten o'clock, they had an excuse ready. All the lawyers at the firm got free massages and psychological counseling. Believe me, they needed it."

"Seeing him get wheeled away in that office chair, with his body slumped over like that, and everybody gawking at him… it's now burned into my brain. It's hard to forget something like that."

150

"If you need psychological counseling, we can arrange that for you," said Audrey. Eric thanked her for this, but he was in too much shock to ask for a free massage as well.

"What's the situation regarding Woody?" asked Eric. "Is he coming back anytime soon?"

"No, he is not. And it has nothing to do with the state of his health. The reason he's not coming back is because there is no such person as Woody Latour. There never was. We received a tip a while back. Acting on this tip, we discovered that none of the educational institutions that he claimed to have attended had ever heard of him. They never had a student by the name of Dagwood Latour. Well, that was just the start. Shortly after this, we found out from another source that Woody Latour is actually Walter Lumley. He grew up in or around Kokomo, Indiana, and according to people who know him, has never been outside of the Midwest. He attended local schools and apparently never set foot in a fancy boarding school. He did have some grade school and high school teaching experience, but it was strictly local. He most certainly never attended Oxford or Harvard or whatever university he claimed he went to. He built a fantasy life out of various influences and he tried to make that fantasy real. He watched British costume dramas on TV, and he read a book called *My Harvard, My Yale,* which was a collection of reminiscences by former students. He indulged in other material of this type, and he created an image of himself as a proper gentleman out of it."

"That's wild," said Eric. "But knowing Woody as I do ... I have to admit I'm not all that surprised. How did you find it out?"

"We know all this because one of his former classmates from Indiana recognized him when he gave a presentation at a convention downtown, shortly before his recent collapse. This classmate joked about it at the convention, saying that it was a matter of concern to him, because his company was thinking of poaching Woody from Eldritch. But when he recognized Walter Lumley, he knew there was no point in going after him. One of our employees heard the classmate's story, and he talked to the classmate and got some more information about Woody. This employee then brought all this information to the attention of management. We followed up. Say what you will about him, Walter was certainly good at spinning a yarn, and his persona as displayed in presentations was very lively. We enjoyed having him speak at conventions and conferences; he knew how to work the crowd. Maybe he should have been a comedian. He was a fraud, but he was a convincing fraud. That's important in business." Audrey stopped abruptly, as if she feared she might be revealing too much.

"Can you tell me who gave the tip?"

Audrey hesitated before replying. "Ordinarily, I wouldn't be able to reveal a piece of information of that nature. But given the extreme circumstances that have transpired today..." She drummed the desk briefly with her fingers.

"Mike did it?"

"Yes."

"How? What happened?"

"I don't know if I have all the details straight, but it was something like this. Apparently, somebody had posted a sign in Italian somewhere in this building, and Woody was unable to understand it. Actually, it was more than that – it was a very famous slogan or some such thing, which anyone who ever studied Italian should be able to recognize. Mike was joking about the slogan with Woody, saying 'isn't that appropriate for our situation right now,' or words to that effect, but it was clear to Mike that Woody didn't know what the sign said or what Mike was talking about. Woody claimed to have a doctorate in Romance languages, so Mike found it suspicious that Woody didn't recognize the slogan. One thing led to another, and pretty soon we were making inquiries to some educational institutions."

Eric sat and stared at her with his mouth slightly open. He wanted to say something, but he couldn't think of anything to say. He put his hands over his face and groaned softly.

"I know that this must be an awful lot for you to deal with. A one-two punch, as it were. Take the rest of the day off. If you feel like it, take tomorrow off too."

Eric dropped his hands. "At my college, there was a rumor that if your roommate died, they gave you straight A's for the whole term to help you cope with the trauma. Anything like that here?"

A faint smile flashed across Audrey's face. "That would be a great incentive to murder the people you work with. No, I'm afraid we have no policy similar to that. But Eric, remember: you get to be the boss now. That is, until we can get this whole situation sorted out. You have to keep the department going."

"Of course I do – there's hardly anybody left! As a content creator, I'm all alone."

"You won't be forever. Be thinking about what you want the department to look like. If you want us to hire another person, start thinking about that now. This is your chance to put your mark on things."

Like a dog pissing, Eric thought but didn't say.

●

Outside, it was early June, the weather was warm and the festive atmosphere of summer was in the air, and the metropolitan area was looking forward to celebrating yet another basketball championship. Sammy Sosa of the Cubs was upping his game in his homerun duel with Mark McGwire, while both of them were chasing the record set by Roger

Maris, back in 1961. All over town, you could still see the posters for another record-smasher, the movie *Titanic*: Leonardo DiCaprio and Kate Winslet happily flying west across the Atlantic, standing atop a ship's mast or whatever it was, joyfully ignorant of the iceberg in their immediate future. *You poor, deluded fools*, thought Eric, looking at them. He huddled inside his apartment, not wanting to go out into the chaotic, capricious world. He had never considered himself superstitious, yet recent events were imposing a pattern on his mind that he could not banish.

First Woody had his heart attack while expounding on his "systems of meaning." He was gone and would never come back to Eldritch. Then Mike had taken over management of the department. He died at his desk, a loyal company servant to the end. This left Eric, by default, at least temporarily in charge of the department.

Eric thought about this with a chill in his heart. It was like the hammer blows in Mahler's Sixth Symphony. The first time the hammer comes down, it cuts off a promising initiative – a modulation to a major key – something like Woody Latour's big plans for Curriculum 21. The second time it comes down, heralding the death of Mike, things are far grimmer; the roaring lament of the instruments lets you know that time is running out. And the third time it comes down ... well it doesn't always do that, because Mahler, out of superstition, deleted the third hammer blow from the final score. But sometimes it gets played anyway, and as Eric stepped into Mike's position, which had been Woody's position, he wondered if the hammer would come down on him. These corporate jobs weren't supposed to be as dangerous as going to war or battling natural disasters, yet here he was, worrying about sudden death or incapacitation while sitting in an ergonomic office chair, with access to as much free coffee and donuts as he could possibly want.

154

•

ExactoTemps was only able to offer one thing at the moment: a day job doing lawn work at a large, ornate house in Evanston. Since there was no immediate promise of office work, Evan took it.

The street, Judson Avenue, was only a block or two from the lake, and was lined with big, comfortable houses constructed with some sense of architectural taste. They must have been several decades old, since they were all different from each other, and didn't have that postwar bland, anonymous look.

It was a two-person job. Evan was assigned lawn-mowing duties. His partner, Jack, would do the delicate surgery, trimming bushes and tidying up the garden behind the house. Jack was a weathered-looking guy with thinning shoulder-length hair and a mustache that needed some trimming itself. Sometimes he would yank the longer hairs into his mouth with his lower lip and chew on them. He wore a T-shirt that was loose except where his protruding belly strained it. He was missing one finger; he didn't say if this was due to a gardening accident or something else.

They got started around ten o'clock while it was still cool. They figured it would only take a couple of hours to do the job, and since agency policy was to pay for at least four hours per day no matter how long one actually worked, it made sense to take it easy. After half an hour mowing the lawn, Evan allowed Jack to tempt him into the shade of the garden with the promise of a beer.

"This ain't so bad," said Jack as they sat on a wooden bench. Shrubs, artistically-carved rocks, and birdcalls surrounded them. "Beats what I was doing last week."

"What was that?"

"Cleaning duty at the high school."

"Yeah? Was that so bad?"

"Nah. I just like outdoor work."

"It's Okay from time to time," said Evan, "but I prefer being inside."

"Whaddaya do inside?"

"Office work, mostly."

Jack smiled (it seemed to Evan) condescendingly. "Gimme the great outdoors any day. T-shirt and jeans, and no asshole in a suit to tell me what to do."

Another half-hour of work, another break. Evan drank water this time, Jack had more beer.

"I played bass guitar in a rock band," said Jack, reminiscing. "Of course now –" he held up his left hand with its missing finger. "Too bad for me I was never much of a singer!" He laughed.

"Maybe you should take up drums," suggested Evan, who didn't really want to ask how Jack had lost his finger.

"Shit, wish I'd had that idea when we were still together. The money wasn't bad, you know." He chewed his mustache a little. "Those were the days. Booze, babes, and…." Jack's voice trailed off; he was probably unable to come up with another appropriate noun starting with B.

"What kind of stuff did you play, and where?" asked Evan.

Jack blustered, seeming totally unprepared for this. "Oh, all kinds of stuff, y'know…some classic rock, some, er, country, uh…bit of this and bit of that, you might say." He didn't answer Evan's second question at all. Evan decided it was prudent to drop this line of questioning.

Jack looked at Evan closely. "So what's your story?"

"Well, nothing as exciting as a rock band. I dropped out of college, and I'm trying to figure out what to do next."

"Hey, I dropped out of college too!" said Jack.

At their third break, the subject of money was explored. The hitherto loquacious Jack became reticent about how he acquired it. Odd jobs here and there, he said, took care of most of his needs.

"I'm not exactly desperate," said Evan, "but I'd like to break into a higher-paying bracket. I'm thinking of taking some computer courses, you know, at community college."

"Think you'd like to live around here someday?" said Jack. "Nice houses, eh?"

"I'm not even thinking about that," said Evan. "I live one step at a time."

Evan went back out front to finish up the mowing. At the house across the street, a garage door opened, and a car backed out and drove away. Since it was a weekday, there was very little activity on the street. Every now and then a car passed through, occasionally you would see a couple of kids on bikes, but on the whole it was quiet.

In about fifteen minutes Evan finished the mowing, bagged the grass, and headed back to the garden to dump it. He felt invigorated by the sun, the fresh breeze, and the newly cut smell of the lawn.

Jack wasn't in the garden. Evan picked up a bottle of water, took a few swigs, and splashed some on his face and hands. He was finished for the day, but wanted to tell Jack he was going before he took off.

He went back to the lawn, where he saw Jack emerge from the open garage of the house across the street. Jack had a laptop computer folded under his arm. Evan froze in place and stared at him as he crossed the street. Jack's deliberately placid demeanor gave way to a sly smile as he approached Evan.

"That'll teach 'em to leave the garage door open," said Jack.

"Uh, what are you doing?" said Evan. He knew perfectly well what Jack was doing, but felt he had to say something. Jack went to the garden without answering. Evan followed him. In the garden, Jack was shoving the computer into

157

the bag where he kept his gardening tools. He shoved firmly but not too hard while grinding out between his teeth the opening riff of Led Zeppelin's "Whole Lotta Love."

"Hey, take it back," said Evan.

"Fuck no."

"You wanna go to jail?" Evan figured an argument based on morality probably wouldn't work with Jack.

Jack leered at him. "What do *you* think?"

"I think you should take it back right now, before there are consequences."

Jack had taken his hands off the computer and was sitting on the ground. His momentum seemed to have been arrested. "You wouldn't rat on me, would you?" He stared hard at Evan, as if trying to threaten him.

"Well, that depends on your behavior, I guess." Evan sat down on the bench. "I don't want to, that's for sure. But I really can't promise one way or the other. If the police file a report, and somehow, the theft gets traced back to two guys working on the lawn – what do *you* think happens next?"

There was silence for a couple of minutes. Jack started chewing his mustache again. From the look on his face he was thinking hard, weighing the options, making predictions. In the distance a small child started wailing. Eventually Jack extracted his mustache from his mouth and spoke. "Okay, here's a deal for you. I won't take the computer. But you have to take it back to the house."

"Why me? You're the one who stole it."

Jack looked thoughtful again. "That's a heavy word, 'stole.' I think of it as promoting public safety. They'll learn not to leave their garage door open again! I've already been there once. Two times is more risk for me. You wanna make the problem go away? A fresh-faced kid like you should bring it back. Nobody will look at you twice. You don't go in, it stays with me."

Evan stood up. He thought of himself as a mature adult and resented being described as a "fresh-faced kid." But he was willing to go along with Jack's plan if it would solve the problem. "Alright." He grabbed the computer out of the bag and marched across the street, through the garage, and into the house. Once inside, he didn't know where to put the computer. He wanted to locate its proper home so as to forestall any suspicion when the homeowners came back. At first, he found himself in the kitchen. The kitchen table was covered with newspapers and plates, as well as a box of Rice Krispies; this was probably not the computer's assigned space. He walked into the living room. In one corner of the room was a small table with nothing on it and a chair in front. This was probably the right place.

As Evan put down the computer, a mechanical hissing started up behind him, followed by the ringing of a bell. Startled, he nearly dropped the computer, then realized that a grandfather clock in another corner of the room was striking the hour. Mission accomplished, he turned and headed into the kitchen. Because of the clock, he hadn't heard the car pulling into the garage.

A woman was standing in the kitchen and staring at him, looking hostile and scared at the same time. She was in early middle age, and right now appeared small and mean, but that might have been due to the shock of confronting an intruder. Evan stopped in his tracks. For a second both of them stood frozen in silence.

With a jolt the woman backed up and shouted "Alan!" into the garage. "What?" came an adult male voice. "There's someone in here!" she shouted.

"I can explain," said Evan.

"Call the police," said the woman, to Alan.

"That's not necessary," said Evan, trying to stay calm. "There was a small emergency and I had to take care of it."

"Are you a burglar or a spy?" demanded the woman.

159

"Neither. Look…"

Alan stuck his head in. He was a handsome, well-groomed guy, probably several years younger than the woman. He was holding a cell phone and examining Evan with a slight scowl.

Evan struggled to exert control over the situation. "The guy I was working with tried to steal your computer," he said, trying to control his quavering voice. "I brought it back. I put it back in its place. Hey, look around. You'll see I didn't take anything."

"Did my husband send you here?" said the woman.

"No. I mean, I don't know. I mean, I don't know what you're talking about!"

Alan had retreated into the garage. Evan heard him talking urgently in a low voice, but he couldn't make out the words. The woman was standing next to a drawer that might contain knives. She might panic and decide to grab a knife and attack him, or (almost as bad) use it to keep him in the house until the police arrived. Evan became acutely aware of how many ordinary household items could serve as weapons in a pinch: bottles, a fire extinguisher, forks, plates…

Evan lunged forward, pushed the woman to the side (she let out a bird-like squawk) and charged through the garage. He dodged Alan, who was still talking on his phone and probably didn't see him coming, maneuvered around the car, and shot out into freedom.

There was an El station a couple of blocks away. Evan ran, panting, across the street, through the garden of the house where he had been working (Jack meanwhile had disappeared) and into the alleyway behind the garden, a narrow strip punctuated by dumpsters, tool sheds, and garages. It was hot now and he felt himself drowning in sweat while his heart beat a war drum inside him. Using the back alley, he ran the length of the block and emerged

onto the street only to be blasted by a sudden burst of water – he had run through a sprinkler.

"Thanks, I needed that," he thought as he turned toward
the El station. It was one block away. At the final street,
Chicago Avenue, he looked up and down. There were no
cops in sight. He charged across without waiting for the
light; an irate motorist honked at him, but he made it in one
piece. As he waited for the train on the platform, he hid himself behind a board advertising a remarkably advantageous
cellphone payment plan. Two very, very long minutes later,
the train pulled up, and he got on it with a moan of relief.

Chapter 14.

Avoid the Void

Eric watched the TV while eating half of a burrito he had purchased at a local Mexican hole in the wall. Half was enough for him; he lacked the energy and appetite to consume the whole thing. The usual subject was dominating the airwaves: the President's shenanigans, a pair of new lawyers for the embattled Miss Lewinsky, Linda Tripp's personnel records, testimony of the President's friend Vernon Jordan, and for some strange reason, Miss Lewinsky's book purchases. Eric had not even followed the scandal closely, maintaining a detached attitude, and trying to avoid the partisanship that had inflamed the minds of so many people. The only firm impression that he took away from it was that many highly placed, successful people were having a public spectacle made of their personal misbehavior, and that this was highly entertaining. He placed the uneaten half of the burrito back in the Styrofoam box it came in, and put it in the refrigerator. The phone rang.

It was his mother. After a few initial pleasantries, she moved on to her usual checklist. "How's the situation at work? Everything okay?"

Eric wanted to convey the idea that the situation at work was not good without causing her excessive alarm, so he smoothed down the sharp edges. "We are in a state of transition. We lost our boss a little while ago, for health reasons. In one sense this is good for me, because it means I have more responsibility. But this year has been frustrating. The company has also not been doing great overall."

"That sounds serious. Are you thinking of looking for another job?"

"I'm not at that stage yet. But I keep an eye out for interesting leads." This last sentence was a lie.

"I'm hoping to get out to Chicago this summer, to visit you and Nora, and a few of my old friends."

"I hope to see you too," said Eric. They finished the call. The longer Mom lived in Colorado, the more distant Eric felt toward her, and not just geographically. Deep down, he had to admit he didn't really miss her. And he suspected that the feeling was mutual.

Intellectually, Eric was aware that the world was an unstable place. But knowing this in one's mind is not the same thing as feeling it on one's skin. The recent events involving Woody and Mike, as well as his rift with Alina, were eroding his mental well-being. Looming over all these things was the questionable viability of Eldritch as an ongoing concern. Previously, Eric was like a person in superb health who reads medical books and websites, considering it useful to keep himself informed, but not really thinking that this information would ever be a matter of life or death to him. Now he was like a sick man, seeing symptoms and dangers all around him.

Insomnia had been bothering him in recent days. Sometimes, it was bad enough that he was afraid to go to bed. The
process of sleep appeared to him as a multilane highway
with numerous exits. Upon lying down and turning out the
light, he found himself on the Highway of Wakefulness. As
he drove with the rest of humanity, he kept an eye out for
the exit to Slumberville. If he missed this exit, he might
get stuck on the highway for hours, tossing and turning on
the Toss-and-Turnpike until he could get himself turned
around and back to the exit, because once you missed it,
there wasn't another for dozens of miles. Searching for the
exit required him to be attentive while driving, but also
relaxed enough to fall asleep. It was a paradox that was
almost impossible to resolve, and if he did fall asleep, he
always wondered how he had managed to do it.

Sometimes it wasn't a highway. Instead, the Kingdom
of Sleep would be located behind a door. Once he opened
that door and went inside, he was fine, but the problem was
that the one door that worked was built into a wall that
contained about a hundred other doors, all of them decoys
that led nowhere. On a good night, Eric knew which door
was the right one, and headed straight towards it without
any trouble. On a bad night, he had to try every damn door
in the wall before finding the right one, and his mounting
exasperation only made matters worse.

The fear of failing to fall asleep was one of the worst
aspects. Eric would lie down and rest like a stone tablet on
his bed, trying to clear his mind of everything. If thirty or
forty minutes passed and he was still awake, he became
afraid that he'd never get to sleep, and fear shot little pellets
of adrenalin into him, keeping him awake for a few more
hours of torment.

But even worse was morning. Soft milky light filtered
into the bedroom. The passing cars increased in number,
and sometimes he heard the *thwack* of a newspaper hit-

ting home, or some maintenance workers puttering about, sweeping and emptying things. Random birds announcing their presence, the bark of a dog, snippets of conversation: these added to the general din. Soon he too would have to get up and start the day as usual, and while keeping busy, would have to find some way to stay awake. After such nights, he always got out of bed with a strong feeling of defeat.

On this particular night, Eric was on the all too familiar Highway of Wakefulness, driving the car that he still couldn't bring himself to purchase in real life. Like all nocturnal travelers, he was looking for the first exit to Slumberville. Tonight something was different: when the exit sign appeared, it said not Slumberville, but Sleepytown. Assuming that they were basically the same thing, Eric got off.

Normally, at this point he fell asleep and stayed oblivious to the outside world until morning. But this didn't feel like the right place. The exit road stretched far into the distance; it was almost another highway. He had the entire road to himself: no other cars had taken this exit, and this alarmed him. It was like a one-way road to nowhere. It appeared that he would have to keep on driving, possibly for miles. The landscape was flat and bleak, like a desert under a cloudy gray sky. Worse yet, there were no signs to Sleepytown, nor any indications of how far he would have to drive to get there. He cursed himself for not staying on the highway as far as the Slumberville exit. Patience was a virtue on the Highway of Wakefulness.

He had been driving for an uncountable number of minutes or hours when he saw a dark shape looming in the distance. It didn't move, so it was probably a building of some kind. As he came closer, it started to look like an old-fashioned roadside inn, with rooms for rent on the second floor and a bar or restaurant on the first. He half expected to see horses hitched outside, as in an old Western. But there were no horses, and the rudimentary parking lot had no cars in it. He decided to stop and ask for directions to Sleepytown.

He parked his car and walked up to the big, knotty, dark wooden door. When he entered, a great void opened in front of him, a vast space composed of various shades of gray. Nobody had to tell him what it was: The Void at the Heart of Existence. At last, he thought, I'm seeing it for myself.

Eric entered the Void. It was dark in there, and quiet. There was a very soft rushing sound. Eric knew that this was the sound that time makes when there are no other factors to impinge on it. He was hearing the very flow of time. He tried to get excited about this but he couldn't.

Inside the Void, it was neither hot nor cold. It might have been up, but was just as likely to be down. The Void wasn't going anywhere, but it wasn't standing still either. Maybe there was a bartender or waiter around, someone who could help him. Eric thought that he should order coffee. Caffeine would help, after another night of insufficient sleep. But he wasn't at work yet; he was still in the Void, and coffee didn't seem to be available. He forgot about asking directions, and decided to stay in the Void and see what would happen.

Soft, repetitive piano music began to play. He tried to ignore it, but it got louder. He opened his eyes: morning again, and his clock radio was telling him to get up. He had no idea how long he had been asleep, or even if he *had* been asleep. Was the Void a dream, or was it some waking vision, containing a special meaning he had to decipher? This was a question he could ponder at work, while irrigating himself with strong coffee to stay awake. Feeling weak, queasy in stomach and mind, and defeated, he forced himself out of bed. At least it was Friday, and he could sleep all weekend if he needed to.

●

Eric thought about the Void and about what it meant to him. It was a feeling he found hard to analyze. It appeared to be composed of approximately equal parts uncertainty, fear, and a general sense of unease, as if the structures of the world were in intermittent danger of being undermined, or even collapsing altogether. He didn't want to think too much about the Void; mostly he wanted to avoid it. "Avoid the Void" was a slogan he could believe in.

He had various ways of avoiding the Void, and on the weekend, he implemented one of them, spending an hour at Pornucopia, checking out the latest in adult entertainment. After his excursion, while walking out of Pornucopia into the sunny street, Eric felt thirsty. There was a McDonald's on the corner. He decided to go in there and get something to drink.

As he waited for the street light to change, Eric felt a looming presence behind him. He turned around. A tall, beefy man was glaring at him, then turning his head to talk into some sort of mobile device attached to the left sleeve of his jacket, up at the shoulder. The man could have been anywhere between forty and sixty, and his ethnicity was difficult to determine – he might have been some kind of Hispanic, or of Mediterranean origin, or possibly Middle Eastern. What was instantly clear was that he didn't look friendly. Eric tried to smile. "Hey, what's up?" he said unsurely.

"I'm gonna have to book you," said the man. "For indecent exposure." Apparently, he was a plainclothes cop.

"What?"

The cop pointed a finger in Eric's face. "Don't 'what' me. You were in that booth, *masturbating!*"

In the space of half a second, Eric's mind became so crowded with thoughts that he was paralyzed. After the half second was over, all he could say was, "This is a joke, right?"

The cop rolled his eyes. "Do you want to come in to the station with me?"

"I wasn't masturbating," said Eric. Always be cooperative around cops, was the thought that went through his head.

"Don't bullshit me. There's peepholes in there. We can see who's jacking off and who's not."

Eric was convinced this was a lie, but it threw him a little. "So maybe I touched my crotch. I didn't unzip. Why do you care, anyway?"

The cop's rock-hard facade softened a little. "You see this building?" he indicated the multistory structure that housed Pornucopia.

"Yeah."

"As long as that dump" – he pointed to Pornucopia – "is there, where everyone can see it, that puts a damper on the value. Things are going to change real soon. Real estate around here's getting hot, you know? You best not come here anymore. And you best tell your friends that too, if they like to spend their time here."

Is this really happening? thought Eric. "Alright," he said, trying to sound contrite. "I won't go there again."

The cop hardened again. "Then let's go."

"Go?" said Eric. "Go where?"

"To the station, fool. For violation of civil code injunction three slash seven oh four, prohibiting indecent exposure in public places."

"I don't believe this is happening," said Eric. His body had gone stiff and numb.

"Do you want me to book your indecently exposed ass for resisting arrest, too?" The cop's voice was quite loud now.

"Shit," said Eric. "No." His mind had left him. He began to fear that other people were listening to this spectacle as they walked past, pretending not to, as people do in such a situation. All he could think was: Always cooperate with the police. Never argue with a man with a gun. Even if he couldn't see a gun on the man.

The cop leaned forward and softened his voice a little. "How much is it worth to you, if I forget all about this?"

"What?"

"How much you got on ya?"

Light began to filter back into Eric's brain as he realized that a way out was possible. He fumbled for his wallet as the cop continued to stare at him. "Uh, let's see." He had to tear at the wallet three or four times to get it open. He pulled a wad of cash out, not even looking to see what it was worth, then thrust it toward the cop. The cop plucked it smoothly out of his hand and counted it in a swift motion. "Twenty-five bucks," he said. "This all?"

"Uh, I think I got a little more." I am never, ever, coming back here again, he thought as he wrenched open the wallet again. Only a few dollars were left. Please, God, make some more money appear...

"Fuck it," said the cop. "This is enough. How you gettin' home?"

Eric had the sickening feeling that the cop was trying to make nice to him, and he had to force down the urge to grovel. "Take the bus, I guess."

"You do that." The cop walked away. Eric stood there, staring into space. Shame and rage battled for possession of him.

Later, while riding home, his head was filled with discordant thoughts. He realized that there was no proof that the unfriendly man was a policeman at all. On reflection, he probably wasn't. Eric lacked the presence of mind to ask for his badge, so how was he to know? He had heard of scams of this type – what might be called public authority scams – but never thought he would fall prey to one. It made him feel stupid and naïve, in addition to everything else.

He reflected on what a foolproof scam this was. Nobody who had been caught and abused the way he had would have the nerve to complain, for fear of having his story made public. "Joe Public had just come out refreshed from an afternoon viewing of *Biff Malibu's Anal Ski Vacation*, when a plainclothes cop arrested him for masturbating in the porno booth. This news was subsequently conveyed to his wife, children and colleagues from work." In Singapore, they had a method of shaming people who didn't flush public toilets. If you failed to flush, a hidden photographer would spring out of nowhere and take your picture; the next day, there was your face in the paper, under a headline detailing your crime. This was even better: just the fear of exposure made people comply. On such scams are real estate fortunes built. It was only a matter of time before Pornucopia went bust. And all because nobody wanted to be caught in public with their pants down.

There was a larger lesson for him personally. Porn had now gotten him into public trouble twice, the first time being his presentation at Eldritch. Remembering his experience at work thus far, and the predictive threat posed by Mahler's Sixth Symphony, he decided it would be prudent to abstain for a while. While he couldn't stop going to work, he could stay away from places like Pornucopia.

Chapter 15.

Lies

Evan Jarrett sat at his desk, revising one of the chapters of *The Positive Life*. It was a morning with no other commitments, the ideal situation for hard intellectual work. On this day, he needed to think even harder than usual. Experiences in the real world had been pounding his careful intellectual constructs with renewed force; he had to rethink some of his ideas.

This morning, he was working on the chapter dealing with moral obligations. His previous draft of the chapter had been influenced by the chapter on altruism. Evan viewed the two chapters as virtual mirror images of each other; it was important to keep their respective contents in harmony, so he was checking his printed draft of "Altruism" against the ongoing work-in-progress of "Moral Obligations" on the computer screen. Evan was wrestling with the problem of mitigating circumstances. In this case, he was concerned with whether "doing the right thing" should be contingent upon a careful weighing of the likely consequences of undertaking such action. If doing the right thing could indeed lead to bad consequences for the doer, perhaps it was better not to do the right thing in the first place?

"I don't need to read anyone to get ideas," was what he had told his philosophy professor, Dr. Frumkin, before he dropped out of college. "I get my ideas from thinking." Later, as he stated in his conversation with Eric, he realized that reading might be a good idea after all. Great thinkers had dealt with precisely this kind of ethical dilemma. Would it not make sense to go to the library and pick up some relevant material?

This train of thought was derailed by the ringing of the phone. It was Ramona Macquarrie. "Hi Ramona. Any good jobs coming up?"

Evan thought he heard a sigh on the other end. "I'm afraid not, Evan. In fact, ExactoTemps is terminating its relationship with you, effective immediately."

"What?"

"You walked off your most recent job without completing it. And as you know, we've had a couple of complaints about you before. We really can't keep you on under these circumstances."

"Well, yeah," said Evan, "but I didn't fill out my timesheet. I'm not asking to be paid for the job." As soon as he said this, he knew it sounded weak.

"But why did you walk away, Evan?"

Just after the unfortunate incident which Ramona was referencing, Evan, understanding the possible danger of his situation, sat down and – in his usual methodical manner – considered how he could put the best possible spin on things when he talked to Ramona. He didn't want to involve the police in any way; they had presumably been informed of the situation, and may have been searching for him. It worried Evan to think that somebody other than Jack might have seen him enter or flee the house. He was certainly determined to stay out of Evanston for the foreseeable future. At the same time, he wanted to avoid implicating Jack directly. Even if he told the truth, it would still be Jack's word against his – and given his erratic behavior recently, Evan couldn't assume they would trust him over Jack. After considering the ramifications of every answer he could give, he settled on the one he had concluded was the safest, and which he could state with confidence. "I got food poisoning."

"Food poisoning? Say what?"

"Yeah, it's kind of an occupational hazard for me. I tend to take food where I can get it cheap. This means free samples from the store, street food, stuff in my apartment that might be past its shelf life. I gamble with food and sometimes I lose. When I was working, I got hit with a fever and then I vomited. I had to leave. I guess my thinking wasn't so clear, I should have called you from the job site."

This self-exculpation was followed by a few seconds of silence on the other end of the line. Evan wondered if Ramona had ever heard such an excuse before. "Evan, I *wish* we could keep you on. I really do, you've got a lot of potential and I think you really do want to work. But we're a young agency trying to compete in a big market, and we need to build our reputation. We've got no shortage of people who want to work for us. We can't make an exception for you."

It was clear that Evan couldn't win this one. The phone call came to an end with a few mutual expressions of regret, Ramona signing off with "I *do* wish you luck." Evan thanked her for the sentiment and hung up.

Evan sat at his desk in silence. He looked at the computer screen, where the chapter on moral obligations was staring him in the face; then at the chapter on altruism, printed out and sitting next to the computer; then at his small stack of business cards, which declared to the world that he was a philosopher; then at the empty box next to the bed, which had contained the pizza he had consumed over the previous two nights. He sat in the chair like a statue, unable to move, for a minute or two. With a sudden jerky motion, he reached out his hand and picked up the chapter on altruism. Swiftly and decisively he tore it in half, then tore the half-pages in half. He opened his desk drawer and took out all the pages of *The Positive Life* that he had printed out thus far. They amounted to about forty or fifty pages of material, and many of them were covered with his handwritten comments. He began to rip these pages up as well; for the sake of variety, he crunched some of them into balls and threw them against the wall. He continued to dispose of the pages until he reached the title page. This would require special treatment. He took a few steps to his kitchen unit and picked up a book of matches. Then he took the matches and the title page of *The Positive Life* to the bathroom. He set fire to the page, holding it up in the mirror so he could watch it burn from both directions, and when half the page was incinerated, he dropped it in the toilet. Then – aiming carefully, concentrating all his scorn on the title, which floated on the surface – he pissed on it. Since he had just drunk coffee, the flow of urine continued for some time, until the words *The Positive Life* were obscured and illegible in the dark yellow flood. Only then did he relax.

His anger was dissipating, and in its cold aftermath, he regretted destroying the pages, because they included his comments on the text. At least he hadn't gone all the way and destroyed the floppy disk that contained the complete draft. After all, it was a good idea to save something for later.

So, what next? he asked himself. Become a hustling handyman again? Sign up with another agency? Go back to school? Try to get a real job?

•

A couple of days after his final chat with Ramona, Evan headed to the local branch of the Chicago Public Library. While he was intending to get a few books on philosophy – ethics in particular – there was an urgent task to get out of the way first. He went straight to the room where they kept the periodicals. By this time, he reasoned, the new editions of the weekly suburban newspapers would be out. There, on the gray metal shelf, he found the one for Evanston and turned to the police blotter. He located the relevant day, then the relevant time of day, and checked the address: that house on Judson Avenue. Although he didn't know the house number, he could tell it was the right block. He expected to find a police report on unlawful entry, attempted burglary, or something along those lines. Instead he read: "Police responded to a false alarm at..." Staring at the page, he wondered if he had the right address or maybe had missed something when reading. But all the details were correct; it was undoubtedly the right location. He was still staring at it when something the woman in the house had said flashed through his mind:

"Did my husband send you here?"

The pieces fell into place. The woman was probably engaged in a little extramarital adventure with the man who was accompanying her, Alan or whatever his name was. Evan then recalled that she had asked if he was a spy. That made things even clearer. And when Alan, acting in haste, called the police, they most likely hadn't considered all the possible consequences of allowing outsiders into their comfortable little situation. Evan imagined how it all went down after he fled: the woman, seeing that nothing had been stolen, yelling at Alan that she didn't want the cops visiting her house with him in it; Alan agreeing with her, and telling the cops not to waste their time.

Lies – his own and those of others – had smothered an embarrassing reality out of existence. Evan, Alan, and the nameless woman were free to sleep untroubled, at least for a little while longer, and to go on living as if the event had never happened.

Chapter 16.

A Proposition

"I wanted to meet with you today because I've got a prop-osition you may be interested in," said Eric. He was buying coffee again, at the same place as their previous meeting.

"What is it?"

Eric recounted the events that had recently transpired at Eldritch: the incapacitation and disappearance of Woody, the death of Mike, the company's need for new blood, and Audrey's encouragement of him to "put your mark on things."

"They actually want me to think boldly, believe it or not, and they're open, at least in principle, to hiring at least one more person to work full time in the department. They've given me a lot of leeway regarding who I might choose. So that's why I'm talking to you."

"Really?" Evan sounded genuinely astonished. "You want me to work for your company? Why me? I haven't even finished college yet."

"Because you need it," said Eric, quoting the line that Evan had used at their first encounter. "No, seriously. You just might be the right person for the job. Look at where the hip corporate culture is being created today, in places like Seattle and Palo Alto. What do we see in those places? We see guys who never finished high school or college, they wear T-shirts to work, they eat pizza out of the box, and they're starting up companies that are worth millions. All because they didn't follow the plan, the whole process of school-college-work-suburbs, the one we were brought up with. Hell, Eldritch is stuck in the 1950s, or maybe it's stuck in Japan in the 1980s, or Europe in the 1960s, I don't know for sure, but we're still wearing suits and ties to work, for God's sake; we're commuting to a box of a building located in the suburb of Boxville, and then going home at the end of the day. We should be eating pizza out of a box like those guys on the West Coast, not working in a box! We need to shake things up. You are one person who can help us do that. Why? Precisely *because* you didn't finish college, for one thing. You dropped out, and you tried to make the world conform to *you* rather than the other way around. Maybe it hasn't worked out as you wanted it to, but in that case, you should try another venue. Perhaps a 'philosopher and activist' is exactly what we need at Eldritch – someone who can shake up the suits. You didn't play it safe, and for that, my hat's off to you. You've done your own writing, you tried to put your ideas into action, you've got a story to tell. Screw the company song, screw college, screw the MBAs and the accountants. Give it a shot, and you might wind up on the cover of *Business Week* in 10 years."

Eric surprised himself with the amount of interest and emotion he devoted to this monologue. He had never talked this enthusiastically about business in general, or about Eldritch as a place with a future in particular. Evan listened with close attention to his entire speech; Eric could tell that questions and comments were piling up in his mind. Finally he responded. "All right, I'm willing to give it a shot. Obviously there is a lot I need to know, like how much will you pay me, what will be the exact work conditions, the job description, all of that stuff. But so far it sounds good."

"We can't pay you a lot, but it will be a decent salary, with benefits. You won't have to eat grocery store samples anymore, and you can start banking for your future in a serious way. Maybe you can still be a philosopher on the side. That's if you get it, of course. I can't guarantee anything at this point. But if I have your permission to talk to Audrey Shroom and a couple of other people, I can make the best case for you, and you can go to the top of my list."

"Okay," said Evan. "You have my permission." They continued to talk about business, and the situation at Eldritch, for a while, until Eric decided it was time for him to take off. "I'd like to get to Vic's Vinyl today, before it closes. It's about a ten-minute walk, so I'd like to leave now."

"I'm going that way myself," said Evan. "There's the cheap electronics store across from there, and I need to get a couple of items for my computer."

•

When Eric walked into Vic's Vinyl, he was expecting to see his old friend Vic at his usual place behind the counter. Today things were slightly different: Vic was at his station, but another middle-aged man was standing there as well. The man had shoulder-length hair (brown but turning gray) and wire-framed glasses, and was wearing a T-shirt that advertised a convention of gastroenterologists that had taken place the previous year, in Berkeley, California. Vic

179

and the man appeared to be doing inventory; a box of records had been placed on the counter, and they were going through it together.

"Paul, why did you take this crap?" asked Vic. He pointed to the box. "There is no demand for any of this stuff, not in this part of town anyway. I mean: 1001 Strings, Liberace, Slim Whitman? I'm sorry, the 50-cent bin is already full. Throw 'em out."

"It's 101 Strings, not 1001," replied Paul. "I thought it would provide a representative selection of historical trends in easy listening music from the early stereo era."

"We're running a store, not an academic library. Into the dumpster with them!"

"Hey there, Vic," said Eric.

"Hi Eric!" he boomed. "We're doing a little weeding out and we have a slight difference of opinion here. Tell me, how much would you pay for this demonstration record of sound effects? Lots of bleeps, ring tones, bloops, crashing noises and stuff of that nature. It's like being trapped in a 1950s sci-fi movie."

Eric took a close look at the record jacket. "That's a historical record that documents how radio used to be done back in the old days, and it also has a certain avant-garde value. It's the sort of record you might play at a party if you're a tech-obsessed nerd who loves noises. I'd give you six bucks for it."

"Hey, the clientele weighs in," said Paul. "What were you saying about the 50-cent bin?"

Vic turned to Paul and said: "Maybe we'll keep a couple of these. But no easy listening, no way. You can go to lunch now. I'll take over here at the counter."

"See you in a bit," said Paul. He put on a light jacket and left.

"New employee?" asked Eric.

"Only for a short time, I hope."

"Why's that?"

"Hah. He's my brother. He lost his job. I agreed to take him on in the store, at least until he gets some good leads. It's something, but he deserves better. Hey, what good are you if you don't help your own family?"

"True enough. What was he doing before?"

"He was a professor. Taught philosophy. You won't believe how he lost his job." In Vic's telling, Paul was a little too large in his personality for the bucolic, low-key atmosphere of the liberal-arts college where he was teaching. Among other things, his sartorial choices seemed calculated to call maximum attention to himself, even while some of his colleagues and students considered them to be excessively showy and provocative. In particular, his habit of wearing T-shirts with messages, graphics, and advertisements, even in the classroom, became a subject of discussion.

"Paul is not a contentious individual," said Vic. "He just needed an outlet for his personality. He was happy with Eastbrook College when he started teaching there. But as the years went by, he started to become more and more discontented. He wanted to move to one of the bigger universities, but the academic job market is dry as the desert right now. They just weren't hiring. He was stuck in place, and his response was that he got more eccentric. He started wearing T-shirts with slogans, or with the names of rock bands, or with jokes. One or two of his colleagues tried to tell him that maybe he shouldn't wear this kind of attire to class, but he wouldn't listen." One day, he was wearing a T-shirt bearing the name of the band the Butthole Surfers. On that particular day, he had scheduled a meeting with one of his female students one-on-one in his office, to discuss a recent paper she had written. The meeting passed without incident, although Paul sensed that the girl was uneasy about something. Shortly afterwards, charges were brought against him for sexual harassment. According to Vic, the student had been so rattled by Paul's Butthole Surfers T-shirt that she had complained to the administration. She stated that she had been unable to sleep soundly and to do her academic work; the image of Dr. Paul Frumkin wearing that suggestive, provocative T-shirt had upset her to such a degree that only harsh punishment of the malefactor would suffice. One thing led to another, and Paul eventually had to leave the college. He threw himself on the mercy of the only person who could help him – his brother Vic.

"I can't pay Paul much, but it's a job. It gives him something to do and gets him out into the world. You know, he actually enjoys talking to people – about philosophy, music, current events, you name it. That's why he was a good teacher. I hope this college suffers for what they did to him."

Eric spent the next half hour browsing in his usual sections. Today he got lucky. Flipping through the classical section, he found the Juilliard Quartet's legendary 1963 set of the complete Bartok string quartets, on Columbia. He had been searching for this one for some time – it had never been reissued on CD, and critical consensus favored it over the ensemble's 1950s mono and 1980s digital versions of these works. The Bartok quartets were the closest you could get to rock 'n' roll with four acoustic stringed instruments; any eclectic listener had to appreciate them, this raiding of the folk music traditions of the world. As Eric made his way to the counter, Paul returned to the store.

"I told him your story!" said Vic. "I knew he'd be sympathetic."

"This really isn't so bad," said Paul. "A nice environment to be in, surrounded by obsolete records and interesting people."

"You probably don't get a lot of philosophers in here," said Eric.

"I don't miss them. I don't need them. I see philosophy being enacted around me, every day, in real life. My focus is mainly on 19th-century German, 20th century existentialism, that sort of thing. If you know your stuff you can see it playing out in front of you. Sartre said that we are 'condemned to be free.' It's a paradox, isn't it – to be free and to be condemned to something at the same time, right? 'Forced to choose,' you know? Or what Heidegger called *Geworfenheit* – the idea that we're 'thrown' into the world. We have to decide everything for ourselves, based on the circumstances we've been thrown into."

Vic boomed: "And how about the paradox of prediction? Everything we do is based on prediction, but we can't rely on that prediction being true. If I get up in the middle of the night to take a piss, I'm making a prediction that the toilet will be there, and will flush. If I get on the bus to go to my job, I'm betting the bus is running, that I still have the job, that the building is still there and nobody has burned it down. When I opened this store, people thought I was crazy. They said there was no market for old records. But I predicted otherwise, and I won!"

"Wait a minute," said Eric to Paul. "Philosophy. Eastbrook College. May I ask what your last name is?"

"Frumkin," said Paul.

"That's a hell of a coincidence. You applied to my company a while back. Eldritch EduWare – we were looking for contractors for our curricular projects. Still are. In fact, I think we talked on the phone."

"Oh, my God," said Paul. "Is that crazy or what? Yes, I think I remember that. We had an interesting little discussion. Too bad it didn't lead to anything."

"I tried to call you. To follow up."

"Well, now you know why you couldn't get hold of me! But what is this, you say you're still hiring?"

"Sort of, yes, but – "

The door opened, and Paul shot a puzzled glance in its direction. Eric turned around. It was Evan. He was standing motionless and staring, a look of amazement on his face.

"Is that you, Dr. Frumkin?"

"What the hell?" said Eric.

Chapter 17.

There Is No Nice Way to Put This

A few days later, it was a beautiful early summer morning in Boxville, and Eric was going through the Routine – telephone, computer, email, coffee. For the first time in a while, he had a large project on his plate: a review of all the material created by him, Mike Riordan, Woody Latour, and a couple of contractors, all of it done during the difficult time of Woody's chairmanship of the department. The goal was to determine what could be saved and what should be tossed. This was a big salvage operation, and Eric wondered if it was even worth it: would it not be easier to throw it all away and start from scratch? But he was not yet willing to subject this task to a purely rational calculation of time and expense. Having spent years working on this material, he resisted the notion of throwing it all away, because he wanted to have *something* to show for all the effort.

Today, he assigned this salvage operation to himself. This was an easy assignment to make: the sole remaining content creator in the department assigning a content creation job to the sole remaining content creator in the department. However, the prospect of having Evan on the team was a hopeful one – someone who could be a great help as they purged the department of the remnants of Woody Latour's malign influence. Eric chuckled inwardly as he imagined how Evan would react to some of Woody's more pretentious effusions. With the road ahead suddenly less strewn with obstacles, Eric was looking forward to the next revision of the material.

As he was checking his email, he noticed the subject line "We have a winner!" He clicked on it and read:

Dear Team,

The management is pleased to announce that we have a Winner in the Eldritch Company Song Competition. The prize is awarded posthumously to Michael Riordan in Curriculum Development, for his song entitled "We're Going Down That Long Road Together."

We are proud to present this award to Michael, as a fitting tribute to his many years of service and dedication to the company. We are sure that you will all be inspired by his example.

A big thanks to all of you who submitted entries. The quality of the songs was high and the final decision was difficult!

"They give an award to a dead man? Are you fucking kidding me?" blurted Eric involuntarily. Some of the cubicle drones nearby must have heard his exclamation, because suddenly there were laughs coming from that direction, followed by a woman's voice saying "you got that right."

The phone rang. It was Audrey Shroom. "Eric, could you come up here for a few minutes please? We need to talk."

"Sure." Eric picked up a notebook and a pen and headed to Audrey's office on the top floor. When he opened the door, he saw that things were somehow different. There was Audrey in her usual place, behind the desk with a serious look on her face; but in one of the two chairs that always faced her desk, corporate counsel David Chiu was sitting. Both Audrey and David said hello in a subdued manner; Audrey added: "Thanks for coming up, Eric. Please sit down."

He did so. "What's going on?"

Audrey drummed her fingers on the desk. "There is no nice way to put this. The upper management at Furuhashi has decided that, in order to realize any value out of their investment in Eldritch, they have to do some serious cost-cutting. For this reason, we are closing down the Curriculum Development department." She drummed the desk again for a few seconds while Eric stared open-mouthed at her.

"That can't be right," Eric protested. "You just told me a few weeks ago that I could make plans for the department's future, and also that I could hire a new person. I was working on that. I even had a new employee lined up. What the hell happened?"

"I'm very sorry about this," said Audrey. "The upper managers looked at the numbers, and they handed down this decision to me. I have to cut what I can cut. There are core functions that any company needs, and I can't cut those. As for curricula, we can license the material from someone else, do some outsourcing, or come up with another solution. Any of those would be a lot cheaper than developing product in house, with a full-time staff that we have to pay for. I know it's small comfort, but yours is not the only department affected – some of the Science people, and the Cross-Cultural people, are also being cut."

"Well *that's* a relief. Suffering together is so much more fun than suffering alone." Eric stared at David. "Are you part of this decision too, or are you just along for the ride?"

David gave him a world-weary look. "I'm required to be here. For the legal stuff."

"David's here because we have to do some final paperwork," explained Audrey. "Eric, you've been with us for three and a half years. We think this entitles you to four weeks of severance payment. You'll have to sign a couple of forms, stating that you are not contesting this layoff, and that you're not going to sue us."

"Fine, give them to me and I'll sign." Eric read through them quickly, just to make sure there was no suspicious fine print. Then he signed.

"We can also connect you with a career consultant," said Audrey.

"What about the psychological counseling and free massages you promised me when Mike died?" This attempt at macabre humor failed; David and Audrey sat there stone-faced. "By the way, speaking of Mike. He's the winner of the company song contest? You gave that award to a *dead man*? What's the prize?"

"Free lunch in the cafeteria for one whole month," said Audrey.

Eric looked at Audrey's serious, guarded face, then at David, whose expression was equally impassive, and emitted a soft, almost inaudible laugh. He gulped some air and laughed again, this time more loudly. As the absurdity of the situation became clear to him, he laughed yet more loudly. David's face registered alarm, and he glanced over at Audrey, who looked back but said nothing.

"I don't see what's so funny about this," said David stiffly.

"Oh Audrey, you are really a genius cost-cutter!" Eric said, wiping his mouth with his shirt cuff. "Free lunch for a corpse. And you know what: I'm willing to bet that

Mike didn't write any song at all. I worked with the guy every day for years, and he never told me he was entering the company song contest. In fact, we used to make jokes about the song contest when it was just me and him in the department. I want to hear this song. What is its release date? And can I buy a limited edition 180-gram pressing of it at Vic's Vinyl, please?"

"Eric, let it go. It's not relevant to you anymore," said Audrey. She looked anxious in a way that Eric had never seen before. It was the nervousness of a person who was used to dealing only with strictly controlled corporate environments, in which every statement, every expression of emotion, was scripted, or at least carefully calibrated not to go outside certain parameters. It was clear that Eric's laughter and comments unnerved her. Eric was tempted to push her further, just to see if he could make her drop the carefully cultivated façade of a polished, presentable professional. He wanted to watch her melt down and say something vulgar and stupid, something that David Chiu would witness and report to other people. He wanted to make a joke about her and the mailroom, the topic that everyone was warned to avoid in her presence. He also wanted to tell David that the open mic nights he hosted at The Angry Ghost were sad clown shows, with only the occasional pleasant surprise, and that he should consider taking up a different hobby. But they still hadn't signed the forms on their end, and he was going to need all the help he could get in the near future.

"Okay," he said. "Sorry about that. I'm cool now."

"We understand," said Audrey.

A few minutes later, when he left her office, Eric muttered: "I am mystified and disappointed by this turn of events." He'd heard that line somewhere.

•

As he walked back to his cubicle, Eric took off his tie and put it in his jacket pocket. It was a violation of the dress code, and sadly, right now that didn't mean much – just another timid, ineffectual gesture of protest. Audrey had agreed to let him linger for the day, but he wanted to get out of the building as quickly as possible; he didn't want anyone to notice his departure, or start asking awkward questions. Cleaning out his desk didn't take long – almost everything in it was disposable and business-related, and there were only a few useful items he wanted to keep (one can always use a couple of extra pens and some Post-it notes). He turned off his computer for the last time and took a final look around at the department. The line from Dante, the one that had triggered the unraveling of Woody Latour's carefully fabricated persona, was still hanging there on his cubicle partition. Eric left it in place, hoping that future generations would benefit from its wisdom.

He went to the entrance to hand over his badge. There was Lydia Walters, at reception; today was the first time Eric had seen her looking sad rather than cheerful or at least neutral. She had probably already dealt with a couple of these departures this morning, and when Eric extended the badge to her, she said: "They got you too."

"Yep."

"Oh Eric, I would never have thought so. You were like a fixture here."

Eric thanked her for the concern, even though the idea of being a fixture at a place like Eldritch was somewhat alarming. "Maybe I can find a better place to be a fixture now."

"Good luck to you. I'm sure you'll find something real soon!"

Eric said goodbye and walked out of Eldritch forever. It was only mid-morning, but there were fewer cars than usual in the lot. It appeared that a few other casualties of today's purge had already left.

It had happened – the third hammer blow of Fate, the one that Mahler deleted from the final score of the Sixth Symphony – had come crashing down anyway. Eric could stop cringing in fear, now that the hammer had knocked him out of a job and smashed his department to pieces, after previously poleaxing Woody and murdering Mike at his desk. Even with the third hammer deleted, the music, and with it the course of events, remained the same – a series of catastrophes ending in darkness. Hammer or no hammer, Eric was doomed either way. With this realization came a sense of relief. In contrast to Mike, he was still alive. In contrast to Woody, he was healthy, and had not been exposed as a fraud. All things considered, his situation could have been a lot worse.

Slowly, he made his way to the local Metra station. The next train back to the city was arriving in half an hour. The sun was shining and there was a light breeze. It was a good day for a long walk, or rather it would have been a good day for a long walk if he had been somewhere other than Boxville. The only reachable local attraction was the strip mall, but at the moment he had no interest in eating fast food, buying a new cell phone, renewing his driver's license, or renting a porn video. He sat down on the platform and waited for the train.

He didn't read on the train journey back to the city; present worries filled his mind and demanded his full attention. One thing he would have to do was call Evan and tell him he wasn't going to work at Eldritch after all. Eric decided to wait a day or two to do this, since he wasn't in the mood to talk to anyone at the moment. He would have to tell his mother, who of course would express disappointment and start to worry. Worse, somehow the news would have to be conveyed to Nora and Porter out in Glenview. Eric tried to push the smug lecturing he could expect from this pair out of his mind. However, he knew the only way

191

to keep them from knowing was to get a new job as quickly as possible. If he did so, he could present it as a personal choice, a positive step that he himself had initiated, rather than a necessity that had been forced upon him. Much worse, he had to consider the very real possibility that he'd be out of a job for months. A combination of savings and (if need be) temporary jobs and (if need be) the occasional humiliating loan from a relative could keep him going, at least in theory. But he couldn't let the property management company that owned his apartment find out about it, as they might refuse to extend his lease, or harass him in other ways.

When he entered his apartment, he was struck by the fragility of everything. He had built a solid life for himself in this place over the last few years. True, guests might be tempted to call it a dump and wonder why a responsible adult didn't take the trouble to keep it cleaner and neater. But nonetheless, it felt like *his* dump, with his own personal stamp all over it. The fact that he now had no reliable source of income brought home the reality that it wasn't his dump at all. The art of downsizing was a subject he had never studied in any detail. Earlier, he had made jokes about how afraid he was that his beloved Rega Planar 2 turntable might break down. Now, he worried that he would have to sell it, as well as the rest of his audio equipment, his television, and any other appliance that was still in working order. Wilson Beefheart at The Book Bunker (assuming he was still alive) would probably give him a fair price for any books he might bring in. It would be painful to reduce the record collection, so lovingly assembled over the years, so richly infused with *sabi*. But if he had to, he could probably cut it at least in half, and he was sure that Vic at Vic's Vinyl would give him a good deal. Maybe Vic would even hire him for a while, as he had done with his brother Paul, the refugee academic. Any job offered by Vic would pay peanuts, but at least it would be something, and in an agreeable environment, surrounded by vinyl records and assorted appealing weirdoes.

But he was getting ahead of himself. There were so many things to consider right now. There was the question of food. A monthly food budget was something he had never made; as a person from an upper middle-class family who had always been more or less employed, it had never been a concern to him. Yet now it seemed not only a sensible but even a necessary thing. In addition to the rent, he would also have to set aside money to keep paying for utilities, while finding and following up on job leads. The question of health insurance would have to be dealt with, and if he couldn't find a new job in a month, he would have to sign up for unemployment benefits. All of this was of immediate importance, something he couldn't put off. Looking on the bright side, they had given him a month of severance pay, as well as access to a career counselor.

There was no reason to panic. He poured himself a big bowl of Cap'n Crunch and sat down on the couch, trying to relax and restore his equilibrium. Stay cool, he thought: it's a boom economy, so they say. Things will work out.

•

"Seriously?" said Evan. Eric could hear Evan's voice cracking in exasperation, even though they were talking over the phone.

"Unfortunately, yes. I'm sorry I caused you to get your hopes up. But everything sucks right now, for me too, and for the whole company."

"I was about to buy a suit. I was even scanning the apartment listings, to find a better place for myself."

"It's a good thing you held back," said Eric. He had waited one day before calling Evan, and rehearsed what he was going to say, in order to sound cool and under control. He didn't want to give Evan the bad news in person, so he called him. "This whole decision was not under my control, and frankly it's the fault of the management. They first told me I could hire a new person, and then only yesterday they told me they were closing the department. They deceived me, and you too at the same time. What can I do in a situation like that?" Evan was silently fuming at the other end, so Eric continued. "Listen, we're both in the same boat now. Maybe we should get together and brainstorm our way out of it. Me, I've got a bunch of things I have to deal with immediately. The shock is bigger for me than it is for you, because I had a full-time corporate job. I haven't been in your kind of situation, where I had to survive off temporary jobs. Not for a long time, anyway. You can go back to what you were doing, right? Me, I have to start from scratch." As soon as he finished saying this, he realized that it sounded arrogant.

"Yeah, well you're the one with the severance package and the counselor. What have I got?"

They continued in this vein for a while. No conclusions were reached and no decisions were made, but complaining and commiserating seemed to help both of them feel just a little bit better.

After the phone call, Evan sat in his apartment, stuck to his chair as if frozen in place. The window was open, and random noises drifted up faintly from the street. The same sounds, the same city, and the same world as before, but now it all sounded bleak and pointless. The feeling of deflation that he experienced the last time he talked with Ramona was taking hold of him again. Only twenty years old, and already he was becoming a victim of chronic unemployment. He knew that he had not actually lost a job this time, but the raising and dashing of hopes felt like a cruel trick, so in a sense it was worse.

He had been reading serious books again, as he had resolved to do not long before. A small pile of them, taken out of the library or bought secondhand, stood next to his bed. A couple of lines by William Blake went through his head: "I must create a system or be enslaved by another man's. I will not reason and compare: my business is to create." From his current standpoint, "creating a system" looked either impossible; or financially prohibitive; or too time-consuming; or downright dangerous. Beyond all these difficulties lay the fact that he still had no realistic idea of what "system" he ought to create. He was still flailing, a young man of no distinction, and without the prospect of achieving any for the foreseeable future. His job loss was merely a component of a larger problem: chronic failure.

Now was a good time to take stock of everything he had done since dropping out of college. He had no close friends – Eric had been a helpful and sympathetic acquaintance, but that was about all. He had no girlfriend, no mentor who could provide useful advice and support (newly jobless, self-absorbed Eric didn't count); he had no siblings, and the thought of admitting defeat and crawling back to his parents disgusted him. Evan did not belong to a church, gym, sports team, high school alumni association, gardening club, reading club, home-brewing club, painting club, photography club, amateur theatrical club, folk-singing club, ethnic food cooking club, bocce ball club, mountain-climbing club, club for philosophical activists, club for college dropouts, club for people who had been thrown out of the house by their parents, or any other kind of club, so he got no support from like-minded, sympathetic individuals. He toyed with the notion of trying to return to Eastbrook College and finish his degree, but the only person who might be willing to put in a good word for him was ex-Professor Frumkin, who had been thrown out of his own job at that very college. His income was meager and unsteady; there were only so many creative ways one could deal with poverty, and he didn't see what other cuts he could make to his budget. He had ceased to work on his philosophical manuscript, *The Positive Life*, after he destroyed the printed copy of it in a fit of pique. Even if he finished it, nobody would ever read it; its influence in the wider world would be nil, as if it had never existed. None of his idealistic actions had achieved anything; he was still the same loser as before.

He picked up the phone and dialed.

"Hello?" said Eric on the other end.

"I've been thinking," said Evan.

"You've been thinking?"

"I'm not sure I should be doing that."

"Thinking is usually a good thing, isn't it?"

"I don't know. Thinking got me into this situation, didn't it?"

Eric was silent for several seconds, then said: "Well, *I* think it's important not to jump to conclusions. Which, if I'm being honest, is my way of telling you I don't have a good answer to that question."

"Here's one thing on my mind. We talked about this, but I don't remember how it ended. You read the book, so you can tell me. What happened to Don Quixote?" demanded Evan.

"Huh?"

"You heard me. What happened to Don Quixote?"

"Why are you asking me this?"

"Just tell me, please. I don't have the book, the library is closed right now, and you're the only person I know who can tell me. Maybe. You read the book, right?"

"Well, yeah," said Eric, "but as I told you earlier when we talked about it, it's been a long time since I read it. He dies at the end, that's the first thing I remember."

"Everyone dies, so that tells me nothing," said Evan. "I'm trying to get some perspective here. Did anything important happen, other than dying?"

"As I remember it ... just before he died, he regained his sanity. He regretted that he wasted so much time pretending to be a knight, fighting windmills, being attacked by sheep and so on. He told people they shouldn't get carried away by their fantasies, or something like that. I remember it was like he sobered up after a very, very long drinking bout. Look, I don't have the book with me, but if you can wait – "

"That's okay. It's enough for now. Thanks for telling me."

"You're not thinking of going up on the roof and waving a broom around, I hope."

"I don't even know how to get to the roof of this building, so there's no danger of that."

"Good," said Eric. "That means I don't have to talk you down." Eric rambled and meandered for a little while, as if he were searching for whatever meager pellets of wisdom he was able to impart. As he kept talking, ideas began to form. "Here's what you need to do. I'm giving you two options. The first one is, you lie down on your bed for at least half an hour, and you don't get up until that half hour is over. During that time, you think about what you're going to do next. That's option number one, the closest thing you can get to sensory deprivation – clearing your mind – in your current circumstances. Option number two is sensory invigoration – filling your mind. You go outside, you wander around, and you get inspiration from that. You look at all those high-rise apartment buildings along the lake, and you think about living in one of them, with a steady job and an interesting life. You look at the beach, and you take inspiration from nature. Or something like that. The ideas will come to you if you let them. So that's my recommendation. Try one option or the other or both."

197

Free to choose, forced to choose. Right now, they were the same thing. "Okay," said Evan. "Thanks."

"Whatever you do, you'll feel better in the morning. And as for me, I'm going back to my beer and movie. It's my way of coping."

Chapter 18.

Hot Takes

"I can take most of these." Roscoe, the eternal graduate student, had just emptied a large bag of books as he stood behind the counter at The Book Bunker. "That's by my count, let's see, twelve, I mean thirteen. I don't think we can sell the others, so you are welcome to give them to the library, throw them in the trash compactor, use them for compost, or whatever."

"You like being the boss here?" asked Eric.

"Hey, it's a job like any other," replied Roscoe. "I never really thought Wilson Beefheart would ever pass. They say it happens to everyone, but with him, I just didn't believe it until it happened. I got the job because he truly wanted someone to keep this place going, and he has no legal heirs and assigns, not that anyone can locate. If he ever did, they probably died back in the Pleistocene Ep-

och. But along with the shop, I inherited Achilles here."
He pointed to the slinky orange cat, sunning itself on the
shelf just behind the shop window. "Do you know Borges'
story 'The Immortal'? I used to think it was about Wilson.
But it was actually about Achilles."

Eric dredged up the only detail from the story that he
could remember. "Do you mean to tell me that Achilles
the Cat was reading Homer in Scotland in the 18th century?"

"Not literally," said Roscoe without missing a beat.
"The entire story is meant to be read as a metaphor for
feline behavior." He zipped up the bag and shoved it back
in Eric's direction.

"So what are you giving me for this?"

"Thirty-five bucks."

"I was hoping for a little more."

"Everyone does. But we can't run this place on 'a little
more.' You'd be lucky to get twenty-five bucks at the place
down the street, but Achilles likes you, so we made a
special deal. Such are the economics of used book stores."

"Okay," said Eric.

"I'll tell you one thing," continued Roscoe. "There is
one book you have, which I can give you twenty bucks for,
if you're willing to part with it. That book is *The Darkening Ecliptic* by Ern Malley."

"No kidding. As I recall, you were pretty scornful of it."

"We ordered it specially for you, and when it came in,
I read it, just out of curiosity. It was fascinating. A real
achievement, even though it was a complete fraud."

"Well, aren't you just full of surprises today."

"Wilson liked it too. It was the last book he read."

"Maybe it killed him."

"Literature has power," said Roscoe. "And to think
those guys, those two poets, invented Ern Malley and
wrote all his so-called poetry in one day. Amazing."

"Sometimes I think that fraud is the only true thing," mused Eric. "Under all the pretty lies and the fake sincerity we have to deal with every day, there is a bedrock of fraud. It's something you can rely on. That means I'm not parting with *The Darkening Ecliptic.* That book stays with me."

•

On a quiet street in a residential neighborhood of Kokomo, Indiana, on a late summer day, a middle-aged woman and a young girl were approaching their home. They were carrying bags of groceries.

"Mom," said the girl, "how much longer is Uncle Walt going to be staying with us?"

The woman looked at her wearily. "I wish I knew for sure, Kathy. He's promised to be out of here by the end of the year. But I don't think his promises mean much. Don't tell him I said that."

Kathy began to whine. "Oh why, why, *why?*"

"Because he's my brother, and he has nowhere else to go."

When they entered the house, they found Walter Lumley sprawled on the couch in the living room, watching TV. Looking like a big, bald, middle-aged baby, he was clad in a red T-shirt with the words *Michigan State* in white block letters across the front. His right hand held the remote and his left hand was submerged in a half-empty bag of Cool Ranch Doritos. An open tub of French onion dip, showing the pits and streaks of consumption, was on the coffee table in front of him. A big bottle of Mountain Dew stood next to the dip, and next to the bottle was a glass full of ice, which Walter refilled with the Mountain Dew every time it got too low. "Hey Louise, hey Kathy," he said, munching.

"Hey," said Louise. "Whacha doing, Walt?"

"Just watching the idiot box." Donald Trump, the New York real estate tycoon, was being interviewed on the subject of the Clinton-Lewinsky scandal. Trump was scathing about how the President had handled the whole situation.

"I think his little speech after it was a disaster," Trump commented. "It wasn't the right tone, and I'm not sure he should have done it. And I'm not even sure that he just shouldn't have gone in and taken the Fifth Amendment and said 'look, I don't get along with this man Starr, he's after me, he's a Republican, he's this, he's that,' and you know, just taken the Fifth Amendment. It's a terrible thing for the President to take the Fifth Amendment, but he probably should've done it. I don't think he could have done any worse than what's happened, it's such an embarrassment to him, I mean I see him walking around, it's like a terrible embarrassment."

"Looks like they're going to impeach Clinton," said Walter. "Can you believe that?"

"Republican assholes," said Louise. She and Kathy went to the kitchen and began putting the food away. "Hey Walt," shouted Louise, "maybe you ought to stop eating those Doritos? I'm about to make dinner. The last thing you need to eat is that kind of junk. Are you trying to give yourself another heart attack?"

"You may have a point there," said Walter. He pulled his hand out of the bag of Doritos and folded it shut, then put the cap on the bottle of Mountain Dew and screwed it tight. "Maybe it's time for me to turn over a new leaf."

Louise emerged from the kitchen. She fixed a skeptical eye on her brother. "How many times have I heard that from you in the last, I don't know, two and a half months?"

"I don't know either," said Walter, suppressing a burp. "Give me credit. I have taken some important steps."

"Like what?"

"Well, I shaved my mustache off."

"That you did. But pray tell, what's so important about that?"

"I'm a new man. I look different. Therefore, I feel different. Therefore, I am different."

"Sweet Jesus," said Louise. "I've got some news of my own. Tonight your clean-shaven 'new man' face is eating whitefish with potato and asparagus. I know you don't like asparagus, and you're not crazy about whitefish, but you have no choice in the matter. That's what I'm making. You can eat it or you can go hungry." She went back to the kitchen.

"Hey Kathy," asked Walter, "you need any help with your homework?"

"No," said Kathy. "I can do it myself." Without another glance at Uncle Walt, she fled to her room.

●

Eric and Alina were sitting in the sun, watching a group of strange-looking naked men with 1960s rock star hairdos frolicking in the water, playing with massive sea shells while they did so.

"It was designed by Carl Milles," said Alina. "He was a Swedish sculptor. They are Tritons, after the Greek sea god."

"I didn't know that," said Eric. "Of course, I don't come here as often as I should. It was a good idea to take advantage of the free day." They were at a table in the Art Institute's interior courtyard, surrounded by galleries on three sides and the museum cafeteria on the fourth.

"I do enjoy contemplating *Nighthawks*," said Eric. "It's such an atmospheric picture. Hopper captures the nocturnal feeling so well. And it reminds me of all the time I've wasted in diners like that."

"Oh, please," said Alina. "The last thing I want to look at is people in a diner at night! I am the person you don't see in that picture. I'm the one in the kitchen, and I am trying to make sure I have the right plate for the right person."

It was only due to circumstances beyond their control that this meeting was able to happen at all. Fed up with her job at the diner, running low on money, and with no better prospects immediately in sight, she was contemplating moving back to Moscow. One of her relatives had a good lead on a job in real estate, catering to the business sector. It was a job where she'd be able to put her increasingly fluent English and growing knowledge of international business to work. All right, she admitted, that bit about her "growing knowledge of international business" was an exaggeration. But it was an angle she could play given the prevailing conditions. While she was considering this seemingly attractive option, the Russian ruble – which had been acting queasy all summer – was devalued, the stock market crashed, and investors lost billions. The expat market shrank; flights out of Moscow were packed with foreign businessmen who would probably never come back. It was exactly the wrong time to go back to Moscow and start this kind of business. The upshot of all this was that she decided to stay in Chicago, determined to give it another go.

"Crazy stuff going on in Russia," said Eric. "I don't think I could deal with that degree of uncertainty."

"You shouldn't think you're immune. Crazy stuff can happen here too, or anywhere. It just hasn't happened during your lifetime."

"I read there used to be churches all over Moscow," said Eric. "Then the Communists blew them up. Changed the look of the city forever. Am I right?"

Alina smiled at his naivete. "It's not only explosions and Communists that make things disappear. You may not know this Eric, but I read a lot of your authors when I was in Russia. When I came to Chicago, I wanted to see the house where Sherwood Anderson wrote *Winesburg, Ohio*. I even knew where to look for it when I got here: on Cass Street. First I had to find out that there is no such thing as Cass Street, now it's called Wabash. But I found the right place. He lived in a house at this address. He got the ideas for the characters from the people who were also living there, so I think it was probably a big house. But today there is no house. It's a parking lot. The house is gone, and I thought maybe there will be a sign or a plaque, telling people that this is where Sherwood Anderson lived. But there was no sign even. There were great musicians on the South Side, Louis Armstrong made his records there. People told me not to go to the South Side, they say it's dangerous, but there's no reason for me to go and look, because Vendome Theatre where Louis Armstrong played is gone. Just like Sherwood Anderson's house. I only know about this because I read a lot. Think of how many people don't know and will never know because they have no way to find out. Or maybe they're not interested."

"Wow, you know more about this city than I do. You didn't come here just for the Al Capone tour. I appreciate that."

"It's my place now. The more I know about it, the better."

"But what's this I hear," said Eric, "about you finding the right guy?"

"Maybe. I've only met him a couple of times, but he seems very solid. A doctor, which is good, and interesting to talk to, which is also good. I don't need another boring guy. Next, I need to find the right job. I have had enough *Nighthawks* for my life."

"Does your doctor friend fit into your sketchbook? I mean, is he eccentric enough?"

"Oh, the sketchbook. I lost it. I left it somewhere accidentally, probably in one of those cafes around Belmont and Broadway. Not a problem, I don't need it really."

205

•

"Our latest brews are Mochaccino Velvet, Strawberry Smooch, and Paint It Black," said the waitress. She had a ring in her nose and her hair was a vibrant, almost electric purple.

"I want coffee," said Paul Frumkin.

The waitress looked at him blankly. "Those *are* coffee."

"Then why do you call them 'brews'? It sounds like beer."

"That's just the word we use for our specialty blends."

"Fine. Please bring me a coffee, as that word was commonly understood in this country before about 1990."

"Got it. Coming right up. And for you, sir?"

"I'll have a latte, honey," said Evan.

"Honey latte?"

"Sorry, I shouldn't flirt. Just an ordinary latte."

"Got it. Coming right up," she repeated, disappearing into the kitchen.

"I like this place," said Evan. "I came here with Eric a couple of times."

"Yeah, it's pretty nice, if you don't look at the cutesy menu items too closely," said Paul.

He was wearing a black T-shirt with no words or images on it. When Evan expressed his surprise at this, Paul told him it was actually a reproduction of Kazimir Malevich's iconic painting *Black Square*. "The T-shirt also shows the artist's name and the title of the painting, but that's in black too, so you can't read it. The great thing about *Black Square* is that it can be whatever you want. It can mean anything or nothing, an oil slick or outer space, a glass of stout or a peaceful sleep. And best of all, you can't get fired for wearing it."

Evan was here to seek advice. One possible way forward for him was to reapply to Eastbrook College and see if they would take him back. Even though ex-Professor Frumkin had left that institution under a cloud of disgrace, he could still be useful as a source of inside tips.

"I no longer believe that the sun was actually revolving around the earth before Copernicus published his theory," stated Evan.

"Well, that's good to hear," said Paul. "Sometimes we need to get whacked in the head by a dose of reality. So how are you gonna make them take you back? I mean, from my point of view, screw them. But from your point of view, it's probably your best option."

"I wrote a philosophical treatise, and I'm planning to present it to them," said Evan. "It's called *The Negative Life: An Experiment in Living*. It didn't take me very long to write it, because I repurposed a lot of material from my original philosophical treatise, which I called *The Positive Life*. My new treatise shows how personal experiences over the last year altered my conception of reality and the principles that I previously adhered to. *The Negative Life* is my way of showing intellectual initiative, creative engagement with society, or whatever the hell they like to call these things. I don't even know if the treatise is that good. But it was a lot more fun to write than *The Positive Life*, so maybe that means something. My parents were impressed enough, they provisionally agreed to pay my tuition again, most of it anyway. Of course, it's good for them, because it means I won't move back into their house."

"I think they'll take you back," said Paul. "The college, I mean, not your parents. It's an okay place, but on the other hand, it's not like you're trying to get back into Princeton. I think they'll be pretty forgiving. And there's also the money angle, which is something they have to consider. I'm still on good terms with a couple of people there. That may help." He looked into the distance reflectively. "So let's say they take you back. You still might want to think – do I really need this? Are you going back to college because you can't think of anything else to do?"

Evan looked at him skeptically. "What are my options? Join the army?"

"It's funny," said Paul, "when I talk to people your age about options, that's the first one they mention. But there are others. Skilled trades. Plumber. Electrician. Anything connected to maintaining a home. You did something like that for a while, right? They can't outsource that, not yet anyway. Just because you grew up in the suburbs doesn't mean you should rule it out. You want to leave your mind free? That's a way of doing it." He slugged down the last of his coffee, then said: "At least, I think it is. Haven't done it myself."

They sat in silence for a few seconds. Then Evan said: "If you could do it all over again – "

"Yeah, you read my mind. It's the regret talking, at least a little. But you should think about it."

Evan asked: "Are you still working in the record store?"

"I'm still there, but I'll be gone by October. I got a job teaching English and literacy skills to recent immigrants. Through a foundation. I tried a couple of community colleges, but they asked some awkward questions about my background. The new job isn't full time, and it's not great pay either. But it's something, or at least the start of something."

"Would either of you like anything else?" asked the purple-haired waitress.

"Sure," said Paul. "I'll have a...oh, what the hell... I'll have a Paint It Black!"

"Got it. Coming right up."

•

208

When Eric moved away from Chicago, he took some items to remind him of his time there. These mementos included such things as an outdated monthly schedule of film showings at the Music Box Theatre, and a beer glass featuring the logo of one of the pubs in his old neighborhood.

One day he was idly paging through one of these mementos, a copy of one of the local alt-weeklies that he had brought with him almost as an afterthought, when he saw something familiar. It was a photo of two robotic-looking individuals standing stiffly at attention, and the caption stated that the phasing team of Dean & Deanna, having just signed their first record deal with a local indie label, was giving a concert this upcoming weekend. Yes, it was the duo previously known as Canned Meat, and before that as Nicotine, changing names as they matured, like a snake shedding its skin. The photo was accompanied by an article, which detailed the twists and turns, triumphs and tragedies, and lucky breaks which this pair of oddballs had experienced in their short artistic career. They were moving up in the world, which was no surprise to Eric. Years from now, he'd be able to say he saw them before they became famous. Bragging rights for him, who lacked anything to brag about – a sad thought.

The phone rang. It was Eric's mother. She had been checking up on him more frequently than before, due to the rapid changes occurring in his life. She was full of advice, concern, and anecdotes – things that were notably absent from her earlier "checklist calls." He appreciated this – the nurse was doing her job properly, responding to a flare-up of his illness, and even making follow-up calls to ensure his recovery was going well.

"Dairy products," she said, with a slight tone of mockery. "How do you like being a salesman for dairy products?"

"No Mom, it's support staff; I'm not selling anything. Not directly, anyway. You do know that companies are more than just their products, right? I'm responsible for staff training, regulatory and legal updates, that sort of thing. I'll be working with the legal department part of the time, and creating some of my own material. Orientation went fine, we seem to like each other. I guess that's all I can hope for at this point."

"Frankly, I'm surprised they took you," said Mom.

"You're not the only one who thinks that. But they were very positive during the interview, and stayed that way after it." In the interview, Eric had surprised even himself; he managed to cast his time at Eldritch in a constructive, even heroic light. According to his sanitized telling (sanitized for his own protection), he was the bold sailor who took charge and steered the ship after the captain became incapacitated and the first mate died. It was only when the ship was pulling into port that the storm arose and sank it. But Eric came out of the crisis wiser, tougher, and more experienced. The interviewers were impressed by his story.

"Still," said Mom, "I didn't think you'd be willing to move out there. You always seemed like a big-city person to me. You're not bored yet, I hope."

"Not yet," Eric said. "So far in this place, the operative word is 'enough.' It's not a big city, but it's big enough. There's not a ton of great stuff to do, but there's enough. The job doesn't pay that great, but it pays enough. I have no complaints – well, I have some, but they're pretty minor – so I'm happy enough."

"Maybe you can finally meet a nice local girl and settle down. Not like that Russian mafia girl you were hanging out with earlier."

"Mom, please leave the Russian mafia out of it. I had my differences with Alina, but you are being unfair to her."

They continued in this vein for a while. After the conversation finished, Eric got off the couch and went to the window to look down on the street from his second-floor

apartment. A couple of people who knew the city had recommended this neighborhood to him. It was a revitalized
former industrial zone, the sort of place where you could live
in a spacious loft in a massive brick building where, generations before, workers had slaved and sweated to manufac-
ture hats, shoes, or now obsolete household appliances. The
workers were long gone, and insouciant young people now
filled the wine bars, artsy shops, and video rental outlets.
It was probably the only part of town where Eric could feel
at home, so it was where he settled. Evening was creeping
in, and people were starting to gather on the street, singly
and in pairs or small groups.

He could see himself staying, at least until and unless
he was compelled to move somewhere else. Maybe Mom
had a point about the "local girl." He hadn't met anyone yet
in his short time here, but she could be out there, maybe
even on that street in front of his building, right now. In
ten years or twenty, there might be the house, the car, the
child or two, the dog, the weekend cookouts, the family hike
in the woods, the touch football games, the parent-teacher
conferences, the church that was neither goofily liberal nor
scarily fundamentalist, the job that paid the bills but wasn't
a great vehicle for personal fulfillment, the neighborhood
friends that you could joke and gossip with while avoiding
particularly awkward or sensitive topics, and the wistful
memory of a now vanished life in the big city that had been
more exciting, and which once seemed to hold a certain
promise: in short, the whole shebang of safe, middle-class
existence. Eric was confident that he could finally embrace
it, sometime in the not too distant future, if he had to do so.
But tonight, he'd lounge on the couch, pop open a bottle of
some limited-edition craft beer, spin a few odd records on
the turntable, and indulge in one of the greatest gifts of life:
a stretch of free time.

Acknowledgements

I express my gratitude to my first readers Bill Hinchliff, Tom Rand, Robert Kingsbury and Laura Freeburn for their helpful critiques and comments. Special thanks go to Tom Rand, urban photographer extraordinaire, for providing the cover photo.

Further appreciation is due to my wife, Olga Uspenskaya, who responded sympathetically to my quixotic quest to get this novel written and published, and to Max the Bichon for his constant emotional support and companionship during the lonely hours of writing.

Thanks also to Jeanette Spires and Lynda O'Connor for their help with promotion. And a big thank you to Krish Singh and the team at Auctus for bringing *Abandon All Hope* to the reading public.

https://swspires.weebly.com/

CPSIA information can be obtained
at www.ICGtesting.com
Printed in the USA
FSHW011542220921

9 781736 827826